By the time he's walked her to the door, Maya had decided—the brush-off. Definitely the brush-off.

As much as she enjoyed being with Wick, she had to call a halt before she became deeply involved. He was too young, too sexy, too distracting, too wrong for her.

She unlocked the door and turned to him. She opened her mouth to tell him good-bye, but the look in his eyes cut off her words. Desire radiated from their golden depths, and his hand reached out to touch her cheek. His gaze dropped from her eyes to her lips, and his mouth slowly lowered toward hers. The first touch was soft, a tentative teasing and testing.

When she sighed softly, his touch changed. His arms went around her and pulled her against him. He kissed her like she'd never been kissed before. When he finally groaned and pulled away, he said, "I've been waiting to do that since the first time I saw you. But it's even better than I imagined. Woman, you set me on fire."

WHAT ARE *LOVESWEPT* ROMANCES?

They are stories of true romance and touching emotion. We believe those two very important ingredients are constants in our highly sensual and very believable stories in the *LOVESWEPT* line. Our goal is to give you, the reader, stories of consistently high quality that may sometimes make you laugh, sometimes make you cry, but are always fresh and creative and contain many delightful surprises within their pages.

Most romance fans read an enormous number of books. Those they truly love, they keep. Others may be traded with friends and soon forgotten. We hope that each *LOVESWEPT* romance will be a treasure—a "keeper." We will always try to publish

LOVE STORIES YOU'LL NEVER FORGET
BY AUTHORS YOU'LL ALWAYS REMEMBER

The Editors

LOVESWEPT® • 443

Jan Hudson
Deeper and Deeper

BANTAM BOOKS
NEW YORK • TORONTO • LONDON • SYDNEY • AUCKLAND

DEEPER AND DEEPER

A Bantam Book / December 1990

*LOVESWEPT® and the wave device are registered
trademarks of Bantam Books, a division of
Bantam Doubleday Dell Publishing Group, Inc.
Registered in U.S. Patent
and Trademark Office and elsewhere.*

*If you would be interested in receiving protective vinyl
covers for your Loveswept books, please write to this address
for information:*

> *Loveswept
> Bantam Books
> P.O. Box 985
> Hicksville, NY 11802*

> ISBN 0-553-44075-6

Published simultaneously in the United States and Canada

---

*Bantam Books are published by Bantam Books, a division
of Bantam Doubleday Dell Publishing Group, Inc. Its trademark, consisting of the words "Bantam Books" and the
portrayal of a rooster, is Registered in U.S. Patent and
Trademark Office and in other countries. Marca Registrada.
Bantam Books, 666 Fifth Avenue, New York, New York 10103.*

PRINTED IN THE UNITED STATES OF AMERICA

OPM   0 9 8 7 6 5 4 3 2 1

*For Anice, Theresa, Sue, Katherine,
and the other pariahs
of the world.*

*And my special thanks to Robin Simpson of
Helicopters International, Inc., for his assistance
and to Raidar Fossen for the ride.*

One

He had cute buns.

Maya Stephens almost gasped when that thought flitted through her mind as she hurried up the steps to the Fairmont Oil Building. True, the male posterior ascending the steps a few feet ahead of her was remarkably taut and well shaped, but forty-year-old psychologists weren't supposed to notice such things. Were they?

Two weeks ago she probably wouldn't have noticed. But two weeks ago, she'd still been thirty-nine. Maybe there *was* something about the big four-oh that made even psychologists do crazy things like buying big scarves with purple fringe or start pumping iron and scoping out sexy backsides. After all, being forty didn't mean she was ready for a rocking chair. Now that she was professionally secure and had put the worst of single parenthood behind her, she was just hitting her stride. She was ready to focus on her own needs for a change.

And he did have cute buns.

The other parts of him weren't bad either, she decided. Her eyes traveled from loafers, up the legs of tight-fitting jeans, over the aforementioned fanny, to the red polo shirt that showed off a trim waist and nice shoulders. The collar of his shirt was turned up in a cocky, masculine statement.

While she was lost in an assessment of his anatomy, he pulled open the glass door and glanced over his shoulder toward her, giving her new data to assimilate. His arms were deeply sun-bronzed, and the dusting of hair on them, like the top layers on his blond head, were bleached almost white. A few strands of his thick thatch, as untamed as its owner looked, fell across his forehead in a careless, devil-may-care manner.

He held open the door and stood back, one hand gripping the edge of the glass, the other resting casually on his slim, out-slung hip. His mustache, a shade or two darker than his hair, twitched on the right side as his mouth curled up in a grin. One eyebrow lifted above the edge of mirrored aviator glasses as if he were conducting his own evaluation. She couldn't see his eyes, but she could feel his hidden gaze slide over her in a blatant perusal that made her skin go hot.

"After you, pretty lady." His drawl was deep with a seductive, gravelly texture that would be lethal in the bedroom.

A flush started at her toes and raced to the roots of her new hairdo. *Bedroom?* Double images of her shocked face bounced off the mirrored lenses of his glasses. She couldn't believe that she, the immediate past president of the Houston Professional Women's Association and mother of a Harvard man, was standing there gawking at this Texas version of a California beach boy and thinking about bedrooms. She might be entertaining the notion of a man in her life, but certainly not *his* type.

Clutching her briefcase in a death grip, she hurried up the last three steps and gave him a curt nod as she strode through the door he still held open for her.

"Thank you," she mumbled. The scent of him enveloped her as she passed. It reminded her of pomegranates and leather and wind in her hair.

As fast as her long legs could carry her, she made for the ladies' room. She wet a paper towel and blotted her flushed face. Maybe she was having hot flashes. No, she was too young for hot flashes. But she was too old for flirtations with sexy young hunks in tight jeans. Maybe the twenty pounds she'd shed recently had affected her hormone balance.

Right now she desperately needed—No! She took a deep breath, then another, and wiggled the staple in her ear. Closing her eyes, she focused on consciously relaxing her body. It didn't help.

Arms propped on the sides of the sink, she stared at herself in the mirror. "Maya Stephens, you're losing it."

Wick McCall drummed his fingers on the arm of his third-row seat and shifted his position again. The No Smoking signs posted on the walls of the small auditorium seemed to taunt him. It had been only half an hour since his last one, but, Lord, he was dying for a cigarette.

He almost got up and walked out. Then he remembered the promise he'd made to his mother. He'd never hear the end of it if he didn't give it a try. His mother had been on his case ever since his father, a heavy smoker, too, had developed emphysema. And he knew he needed to quit. Everywhere he turned nowadays there was another reminder of the evils of nicotine.

Rubbing his palms on his denim-covered thighs, he looked around the room, trying to distract his thoughts from the craving invading his mind and muscles. The seventy-five or so plush seats were arranged in tiers like a teaching theater, and something about the feel of the place reminded him of the strict regimentation of his old high school. Those days had been more than twenty-years ago, but, even now, the impression made him want to cut and run.

He swiped his hand over his face to erase the disquiet and studied the people gathered. About half of the chairs were occupied. He didn't know a soul there, which wasn't surprising. He wasn't an employee of Fairmont Oil. Doug Hastings, an old diving buddy and director of human resources for Fairmont, had invited him.

"I promise you," Doug had said, "hypnosis is the most painless way to quit. This psychologist is phenomenal. She conducted a series of sessions for us last spring, and ninety percent of the people who participated are still off cigarettes. Look at me; I'm a prime example. It's time you gave up the filthy habit."

Wick scowled and drummed the fingers of the other hand. There was nothing more self-righteous than an ex-smoker. He squirmed in his chair and looked at his watch. If she wasn't here in the next sixty seconds, he was leaving.

In exactly fifty-eight seconds, the door opened and a tall redhead strode in. Wick sat up straight.

She put her briefcase on the desk in front, and he sat up even straighter. This was the woman he'd noticed outside, the one he'd held the door for.

Her eyes scanned the room, hesitated for a heartbeat when they rested on him, then moved on. His gaze stayed on her. Surely this lovely lady with the sultry green eyes, lush lips, and lusher curves wasn't the psychologist.

She smiled. "I'll bet a lot of you are dying for a cigarette about now." After a few nervous laughs and some foot shuffling from those assembled, she crossed her arms and leaned back against the desk. In a low, resonant voice she said, "If you think you absolutely can't make it through the next forty-five minutes without a cigarette, you can go outside and grab a few puffs. We'll wait for you."

She looked around to see if there were any takers. There was some more foot shuffling, but nobody got up. She smiled again, uncrossed her arms, and stepped forward. "Good for you. I think you're serious about this. I'm Dr. Maya Stephens. I'm a clinical psychologist and a hypnotherapist. How many of you have been hypnotized before?"

A few hands went up. She nodded. "Good. I'll ask you to share your experiences with us in a moment. I suspect that many of you are a little anxious about being hypnotized. You've probably seen stage hypnotists on television who make people do weird things. I don't do any of that kind of stuff, and I promise not to make a single one of you act like a chicken or a washing machine."

After pausing for chuckles from the group, she asked, "What do you think it feels like to be hypnotized?"

While several people ventured an answer, Wick

listened with only a part of his attention. The rest of it was busy checking out the good doctor. Now this, he thought as he studied her, was a woman. Good legs from what he could see below the full skirt. The two-piece knit dress she wore was loose, but as she moved, the soft, moss-green fabric hugged a dynamite figure with full breasts and enough curve to her hips to qualify as voluptuous without being overblown.

Her face had an exotic cast to it. And even with deep red—really auburn-colored—hair not a freckle marred her olive-skinned beauty. She had the kind of high cheekbones, strong chin, and full mouth that would never be considered cute. Striking, he decided. She was striking.

"Hypnosis is nothing more than following suggestion," she said. "Let's do a simple exercise to demonstrate. Close your eyes and hold your arms straight out in front of you. Imagine that you have a bunch of helium-filled balloons in one hand and a bucket with a rock in the other."

Wick dragged his attention to the task and gamely joined in with the group. He followed her directions to add imaginary balloons to his right hand and more rocks to the bucket in his left one.

"Now open your eyes," she said. "Look at your arms. Do you see a difference? Do you feel a difference?"

Well, I'll be damned, Wick muttered to himself. His right hand was a good five inches higher than his left. He flexed his arms. The left one seemed more strained, as if he'd really been holding a weight.

A general buzzing traveled around the room as people compared their experiences. Maya Stephens stood watching and smiling until they were quiet. He noticed that she didn't look at him.

"Amazing, isn't it?" she asked. "I didn't do anything except make suggestions. *You* concentrated and used your own imagination to follow my suggestions because you chose to. That's what hypnosis is. A relaxed state using concentration, imagination, and suggestion."

Stepping away from the desk, she moved close to those in the front row and casually slipped her long fingers into the pockets of her skirt. Before her hands were out of sight Wick noted that the only ring she wore was a large, intricately wrought gold one on her left index finger.

"This afternoon we're not going to worry about smoking. I'm going to teach you to relax through suggestion, and I've brought some tapes for you to use at home. If you decide to continue, we'll meet for about an hour on Monday and Thursday afternoons for three weeks. Any questions?"

As she answered questions and allayed some of the fears people expressed about being hypnotized, Wick sat quietly and watched her. She was charming the socks off of everybody there with her gentle humor and confident manner. He was impressed.

"Now let's get to the relaxation. Kick your shoes off if you want, loosen ties and belts, take off your jacket if you'd like. Wiggle around and get comfortable. Take a deep breath and close your eyes. Imagine yourself, if you would, on a beautiful beach. It's quiet and peaceful . . ."

He closed his eyes, and the silkiness of her voice poured over him like warm honey. He was stretched out on white sand, soft and warm against his body. Sea gulls circled and called above his head, and a light breeze ruffled his hair and whispered over his skin. He took a deep breath, and he could smell salty air and feel his tension melt like butter and run into the sand beneath him. Gentle waves lapped the shore, and with their ebb and flow he went . . .

"—deeper and deeper into very relaxed feelings. Feeling so good and so relaxed."

Like the lull of a Lorelei, her contralto was compelling, soothing. There was no one in the world but the two of them as he listened to the most sensuous sounds he'd ever heard. Drifting into his own fantasy, he ignored her directions and concentrated only on the tempo and texture of her words. The erotic fingers of her voice stroked his face, his chest, his belly. Her breath replaced the breeze as her full lips and velvety tongue gently moved over his boneless body from toes to forehead. Her auburn hair, long, full, and flowing, grazed his sun-warmed skin as he went . . .

"—deeper and deeper into very relaxed feelings. You feel so good and so relaxed."

In his fantasy her eyes were sea-green and heavy lidded, and the sun sparked her hair to copper fire as she bent over him and wove her magic with sibilant sounds and languid touch. Her skin was sun-drenched satin, and her smile was a siren's smile as she lowered her lips to his. Their tongues met and his hands ached to slide over full, creamy breasts and along the lush curve of bare hips. But he couldn't move. He could only lie there and listen to her sexy voice weave its wondrous spell.

Every part of his body was relaxed except one, and it was growing less and less relaxed. He tried to lift his arms to wrap them around her, but the muscles wouldn't obey his command. She pulled away and, giving him a sultry smile, rubbed her palms over his chest with long, slow strokes. She murmured soothing words, straddled him with her long legs, and began to lower herself . . .

"—deeper and deeper. You've never felt so good. You feel won-der-ful."

Holy hell! one part of his mind said, *this is only your imagination.* Another part told the first part to get lost. This felt damned good. She flung her head back and rotated her hips slowly as she encased more and more of him in her tight, wet heat. Sweat popped out on his forehead as she sank . . .

"—deeper and deeper."

Snap out of it, McCall, before you embarrass yourself in front of all these people. More sweat popped out.

"It feels so good to lie there on the beach with your eyes closed. Your eyelids feel as if they are glued shut, because you can't open them. Try to open your eyes."

The damned things wouldn't open! He strained and strained, but it felt like somebody had squirted glue in his eyelashes.

"Just relax," she crooned. "Your eyes are perfectly normal. I'm going to count to five and you're gong to come wide awake. You're going to feel wonderful. Relaxed and refreshed, but perfectly normal and alert. And you're going to sleep so well tonight. With a big smile now—one . . . two . . . three . . . four . . . five. Wide awake."

He grinned as his eyes popped open. She was looking right at him, smiling. He was still aroused. Lord, she was the sexiest woman he'd ever met. That voice of hers turned him on like a house afire. He meant to change his fantasy into the real thing at the earliest opportunity.

Breaking eye contact with him, she turned quickly to the others who were blinking and smiling. "Feel relaxed?" she asked the group. "That's what it's like to be hypnotized. Nice, hmmm?"

Nice didn't begin to describe what he was feeling. He squirmed in his chair.

"Now that you're more comfortable with the idea, we'll go even deeper next session. Any questions?"

"Yeah," a man on the front row said. "What's your phone number, darlin'?" He took the words from Wick's mouth.

She looked amused. "Now you wouldn't want to jeopardize my license, would you? I don't date clients." She laughed. "And I *never* go out with men who smoke."

Everybody laughed at her good-natured bantering with the wise guy, but Wick felt like he'd been hit in the head with a sack of rocks.

As she wound down the session and passed out the tapes she'd brought, he stayed in his seat, giving his blood time to cool and trying to come up with an excuse to ask her out. And he intended to see more of her. A lot more. He'd have to come up with something good. He'd never met a female he couldn't talk his way around, but this lady was sharper than most. She far outclassed the airheads who hung out at the swimming pool at his apartment building. Not only was she bright and sexy, but her warmth and sense of humor appealed to him. In fact, there was something vaguely familiar about her. Yet, he couldn't remember ever having seen her before. It puzzled him.

Suddenly, he captured the elusive memory. Miss

Bergstrom. He shook his head and smiled to himself as he thought of his turbulent teenage years. He'd been all zits and rebellion at sixteen. Brash, sullen, and impatient, he'd been an explosion looking for a place to happen.

He'd hated the boredom and restriction of high school, hated his classes, hated his teachers, and hated his parents. On the verge of flunking his junior year, he'd been ready to drop out of school and leave home when Laura Bergstrom, the school counselor, got hold of him and wouldn't give up. Under her patient guidance, he'd straightened out—at least enough to endure Odessa High until graduation. And he'd developed a huge crush on her. He'd mowed her lawn, washed her car, and adored her with all the secret passion and fantasy of adolescence. Because of her, he'd opted for college instead of the marines. For years afterward, he'd measured women against Laura Bergstrom. No one had ever come close.

But he was a big boy now, and Maya Stephens was no unattainable Miss Bergstrom.

When the crowd thinned out, Wick got up and sauntered down to where she was standing. He hung back until she had passed out tapes to the last of them.

She smiled and held out a tape to him. "Here you go."

"Thanks," he said, taking it. "But I have to admit I'm here under false pretenses."

Her eyebrows lifted. "Oh?"

He grinned. "I haven't had a cigarette in a long time." Hell, he wasn't lying. An hour and a half *was* a long time for him. "I'm interested in a program like this for my company." He pulled a business card from his wallet and handed it to her. "Doug Hastings is a friend of mine, and he invited me to sit in. I'm impressed with your work. I'd like to discuss your doing this for my employees. Are you free for dinner tonight, Dr. Stephens?"

Maya hesitated for a moment before she spoke. Years of clinical practice allowed her to maintain a calm facade, but she felt like a swarm of bees had been loosened inside her. Raw male virility and sexual awareness radiated from this man like a fever. It pulsated. It warmed the air around him.

Because they were hidden earlier by sunglasses and later by distance, she hadn't seen his unusual eyes. She was mesmerized by them now. With deep lines fanning out from the corners, they were the tawny gold of a tiger's and permanently narrowed into the same predatory slits, worldly wise and waiting. They challenged and taunted and missed nothing.

She'd have to be nuts to get mixed up with him.

"I'm sorry, Mr.—" She looked down at the card.

"McCall," he supplied. "Wick McCall."

He gave her a lazy grin and one flick of those narrow gold eyes. A sexual shock wave flooded her brain. Adrenaline poured into her bloodstream. Her first impulse was to give in to her primitive fight or flight system and run like crazy. She forced herself to stand her ground.

"I'm sorry, Mr. McCall, I'm not free this evening. And my schedule is so full for the rest of the year that I don't think I can take on any more companies. However, I'll be happy to recommend another of my colleagues."

He shook his head. "I want you."

Maya was extremely perceptive, but it didn't take a Ph.D. to discern his motives now. She was very sure that he was suggesting more than a business relationship. That's what she got for ogling men's buns. She had a tiger by the tail, and she didn't know what to do with him.

"I'm sorry," she said. "Now, if you'll excuse me, I have to get back to my office for an appointment." She grabbed her briefcase and fled the room.

Walking out of the building and across the parking lot at a fast clip, she was still shaken by the experience. In the seventeen years since Ron's death, she'd never encountered a man who affected her at such a visceral level. She'd long ago accepted that what she and Ron had shared was a once-in-a-lifetime thing, a product of the fervor of youth and the agitated state of the world. She'd never expected to encounter anything like it again. In truth, she didn't know if she could handle such intensity at this time in her life.

Granted, she had made some changes. Between her sister-in-law Chelsea's badgering and forty staring her in the face, Maya had decided to embark on a self-improvement, self-indulgent kick. A little hedonism was good for the soul, she reasoned. But her project wasn't begun with the sole intention of catching a man. True, with her son, David, gone, her other-centered, celibate life had become a bit boring. And the thought had crossed her mind to cast her net among the few available males in her age group. But she had figured on finding a nice middle-aged doctor or banker type— *not* a tiger in tight jeans.

She'd be damned if she'd become one of those middle-aged women who wore too much rouge and flirted with lifeguards. No, a nice banker type would suit her fine.

A few minutes later she sat in her ten-year-old

station wagon grinding on the ignition and wiggling the staple in her ear. Neither of her efforts produced any noticeable results.

"Having problems?"

She was startled at the deep voice and jerked her head around to find Wick McCall casually draped over the door of the passenger side, his head stuck inside.

"My car won't start."

"Smells like it's flooded. Pop the hood and I'll check it out."

After a few minutes under the hood, he slammed it down and, wiping his hands on his handkerchief, ambled back to where she sat fuming.

"It's flooded. Just let it sit for a few minutes and it'll probably kick over. Looks like you could use a new carburetor."

"I could use a whole new car." She made a derisive sound. "But I don't have a few minutes. I have a client due"—she checked her watch—"right now."

He opened the door. "Come on. I'll drive you."

She almost refused but decided it would be stupid. "Thank you." She climbed out, dragging her briefcase with her.

He reached in for her car keys and dangled them in front of her. "Don't you want to lock it?"

She curled her lip in disgust. "If anybody wants to steal it, they're welcome to it."

Laughing, he shepherded her to a Corvette, very low and very red. There was no way to get into the thing gracefully, but she gave it her best shot.

When they were strapped in, he asked, "Which way?"

She pointed. "Five minutes that way."

"I'll have you there in three." The powerful car roared from the parking lot.

"I really appreciate the lift, Mr. McCall."

"Call me Wick."

"That's an unusual name. Is it short for something?"

"Yeah." He glanced over at her, grinned, and winked one tiger's eye. "Wicked."

Two

Maya thought the elevator would never reach the fourth floor. She was a nervous wreck and jiggling that damned staple didn't do a bit of good. When the stainless steel doors parted on her stop, she shoved her way from the rear and charged down the hall.

Two doors before her office, she ducked into a broom closet. She stubbed her toe on a mop bucket and hissed a blistering oath as she scrounged through her case. Mr. Brooks was probably waiting for her, but he could wait another two minutes. She couldn't.

In the top pocket, she found two crumpled cigarettes, one cracked in the middle and barely hanging together, and a pack of matches. She grabbed the more mangled one and ripped off the broken part. She crammed the filter tip in her mouth, lit it, and took a long drag.

It was heaven.

After another few quick puffs, she turned to the wet gray mop propped against a wall. "Yes, I feel like an idiot. Yes, I feel like a hypocrite. Yes, this is a hell of a way for a grown woman to act."

The butt sizzled in the dirty mop bucket. She sprayed her mouth with spearmint breath deodorant, opened the door, and used the private entrance to her office.

Her secretary of eight years, Camilla Davis, glanced up as Maya came in. "Mr. Brooks is waiting," Camilla said as she followed Maya into her office.

"I figured as much." Maya put away her case and took a deep breath. "Send him in."

"Chelsea called and asked you to pick up a couple of lamb chops on your way home, and Dr. Younger needs to talk to you about one of his patients." The tall black woman with a graying Afro leaned over and sniffed. "Smells like you fell off the wagon again."

"Camilla," she said, narrowing her eyes, "stow it."

After she spent a full hour with Mr. Brooks's cynophobia—his fear of dogs—a real problem since his fiancée had a German shepherd, two poodles, and a Lhasa apso that were like children to her; and another hour with a young mother who was suicidal, plus twenty minutes consulting with Dr. Younger about a borderline personality, Maya was pooped. It had been a long day.

And she wanted a cigarette. A few puffs stolen in the broom closet didn't cut it. She wiggled the staple in her ear. It didn't help. She kicked off her shoes and was about to slip one of her own tapes into the cassette player on her desk when Camilla buzzed her.

"Yes?"

"Chelsea called. She said to forget the lamb chops for dinner; she's got a hot date and won't be in until late. Dr. Adams's secretary called and said that tonight's meeting has been canceled and will be rescheduled for next week. Dr. Adams went home with the flu. Looks like you're going to have a quiet night, boss."

Yes, and the first thing I'm going to do is stop and buy a pack of cigarettes and smoke every one of them.

"And," Camilla added, her voice dropping an octave, "there's a Mr. McCall here to see you. He says it's something about your car."

"McCall? Wick McCall?"

"Tall blond hunk with a mustache. If I were you, I'd lock myself in with him and throw the key out the window."

Maya heard a masculine laugh in the background. "Camilla! Did he overhear what you said?"

"He's standing right here. I expect he did unless he's deaf, but he looks to me like *all* his parts are working. Want me to send him in?"

"Remind me to fire you next week." Maya sighed and Camilla laughed. "Yes, send him in."

She was trying to find her other shoe when Wick appeared. He looked around, his gaze passing quickly over the area, that, except for her desk, was furnished like a comfortable living room with a mixture of traditional, contemporary, and oriental styles. Even with his quick, casual perusal, she could tell he didn't miss anything from peach carpet to pre-Columbian art collection.

The lines around his eyes crinkled as he gave her a slow smile. "I like your office. Nice, restful." He walked over to one of the walnut bookcases lining one wall and picked up a small figure from among the assortment of bowls and other carved and painted vessels. "Except for this fellow. Who is he?"

Her toes searched under her desk for the missing pump. "A Mayan warrior, about 600 A.D."

His blond eyebrows went up. "Mayan, Maya, like your name."

"My parents are archaeologists. They were on a dig in Central America when I was born." Her toes fanned out to widen their search. "Well, I wasn't exactly born on the dig site. My mother did stop long enough to go to the hospital."

He walked over, squatted beside her, and peered under her desk. His arm brushed her leg as he reached into the opening. She flinched and rolled her chair back.

"This what you're looking for?" He held up a camel-colored pump.

She nodded. He picked up her ankle, and she held her breath as she felt his fingers against the back of her lower leg.

His gold eyes locked with hers, and he slipped the shoe on her foot. "It fits. You must be the lady I've been scouring the countryside for." He continued to hold her ankle.

"Pardon?"

He laughed. "Didn't you read *Cinderella* when you were a little girl?"

"Oh." She forced a nervous chuckle. "Of course." She tugged at her foot, but he didn't let go. "What are you doing here?" she blurted out.

He released her ankle and stood. "I got your car running, but I had to replace the carburetor. It's parked downstairs in the lot."

"You didn't have to do that."

"I wanted to."

"I'll pay you for it." She reached for her check-book. "How much do I owe you?"

"Have dinner with me tonight, and we'll call it even."

"I prefer to give you a check." She didn't want to be in his debt, and she didn't want to play subtle blackmail games.

He smiled. "And I'd prefer to take you to dinner. Since Chelsea canceled the lamb chops, and Dr. Adams has the flu, I know you're free."

Right now she could cheerfully strangle that blabbermouth of a secretary. "Did it ever occur to you, Mr. McCall, that I might not want to go out with you?"

"Wick." He flashed another grin. "The thought crossed my mind. I ignored it." He reached for her hand and hauled her to her feet. "Come on, give me a couple of hours. Strictly business. Besides, I need a lift back to my car. There's a Mexican restaurant on the next block. Like Mexican food?"

"I'm on a diet."

"Boy, you're hard to please. Okay, there's a seafood place on the way. We'll stop there."

She only had time to grab her purse before he took her arm and spirited her from her office. "I'll see you in the morning," she called to her secretary over her shoulder.

"Thanks, Camilla." He gave the grinning woman a big wink and a thumbs-up sign before he closed the door.

Frowning, she asked, "What was that all about?"

"Oh, Camilla and I became buddies while I was waiting for you. She told me all sorts of interesting things about her boss. Like—"

An elevator opened, and they were quiet as they

rode down with two men in business suits and a woman holding a baby. What had Camilla told him? The first thing in the morning, Maya was going to give her secretary a stern lecture about invasion of privacy and employee responsibility.

Wick had helped her into the passenger side of her own car and gotten behind the wheel before he spoke. "Why the frown?"

"My secretary knows how important confidentiality is in our office. She's usually the soul of discretion."

He laughed. "She didn't say much really, except that you're a widow and you work too hard." The station wagon purred to life in a way it never purred for her, and he pulled away. "Who's Chelsea?"

"My sister-in-law. My husband's youngest sister. She's been living with me since her divorce about a year ago. She goes to law school and works part-time."

"How long have you been a widow?"

"Seventeen years."

"Vietnam?"

She nodded.

"Any kids?"

"I have a son, David, who's a sophomore at Harvard. And you?"

"I've never been married."

She wanted to ask him how old he was and why he wasn't married, but she bit her lip and was silent. What possible difference did it make? He was simply a man who'd fixed her car and was taking her to dinner to talk business. Forget the physique. Forget the sexy smile and tiger eyes. Forget the masculine aura that filled the car nearly to bursting.

She desperately craved a cigarette.

When they went inside the restaurant, she spotted a cigarette machine in an alcove between the rest rooms. After they were seated in the non-smoking section and she'd ordered a glass of white wine to his bourbon and water, she excused herself to "powder her nose."

"Mine needs powdering too." He rose and followed her.

Damn! They parted at the cigarette machine and went in separate doors. As soon as she was inside, Maya grabbed her wallet and cursed again when she discovered only two quarters and a penny in coins and no bill smaller than a five. She'd have to get change. With a five in her hand and her purse under her arm, she shoved open the door.

Wick was standing by the cigarette machine. He glanced up. "Just getting some gum." He pulled a knob and a package slid out accompanied by the jingle of coins being returned. "Need something?" He scooped up gum and coins.

"I, uh, need some change from the cashier. For, uh, in there."

She waved her hand in the general direction of the ladies' room.

"How much you need?" He dug in the pocket of his tight jeans.

"Five quarters."

His eyebrows lifted. "Must have gone up." When she stared at him blankly, he grinned. "I have three older sisters and four nieces. I'm used to all kinds of female stuff."

After a second, it dawned on her what he was talking about. If she'd been the blushing type, she would have blushed. Luckily, she wasn't. Determined to brazen it out, she did nothing to correct his misperception. "Do you have change?"

He opened his hand, and she took five of the six quarters which lay on his palm. "Thank you." Turning, she went back in the ladies' room.

She leaned against the wall and gave a sigh of disgust. This was ridiculous. An adult shouldn't have to behave this way. Yet, here she was sneaking around like a teenager. This was stupid, absolutely stupid.

Cracking the door a hair, she peered through the tiny slit. All clear. She ran out, poked Wick's five quarters and her two into the slot, and pulled the knob. Snatching up the package, which promised the lowest tar and nicotine, she ran back into the ladies' room, unwrapping as she went.

Ignoring the No Smoking sign, she stuck a cigarette in her mouth and dug through her clutch bag for a light. Finally, she came up with a dogeared folder advertising tractors. Where it came from, she had no idea.

Empty. Her shoulders slumped. Were the Fates conspiring against her? She shoved the package in her purse and went out the door. Surely there were matches at the register. Every restaurant had them.

Wick was standing in a cluster of people by the cashier. He started when he saw her, then smiled. "Ready for your drink now?"

She ground her teeth together. "Yes, thank you." Her back stiff, she strode to their table. Wick picked up his drink, which looked a little watery on top, and held it up for a toast. She didn't even hear what he said as their glasses clinked together, for, three tables away in the smoking section, she could see and smell glorious plumes of smoke wafting upward to the acoustical ceiling tiles.

She breathed deeply, trying to enjoy vicariously what she had been denied in reality. It wasn't the same. Her stomach cramped.

In three big gulps her wine disappeared. "Order me another, please." She clunked her glass on the table. "I need to make a phone call."

Before he could say a word, she was gone. Appropriating a matchbook on her way, she charged into the ladies' room. Two women in polyester pants, very loud and very obese, stood at the double sink. One was brushing her long black hair, and the other was splashing water on her hands. Maya ignored them as she pulled out a cigarette and lit it.

She inhaled a deep drag, held it, then slowly let it out. It was bliss. Another puff, and her muscles relaxed.

"You're not supposed to smoke in here," a nasal voice whined. "Don't you see the sign?" The one with the hairbrush glared at her.

Maya glared back and said in her most quelling professional tone, "This is an emergency."

"Well, I never," the hand washer said. "Some people are *so* inconsiderate." She threw a wad of soggy towels on the floor and marched out with the hairbrusher on her heels.

After a few more puffs, Maya flushed her cigarette down the toilet and walked to the sink. She picked up the towels from the floor, dried the water-splashed counter, and wiped away the long black hairs in the sink as penance for her sin.

When she returned to their table, the chair behind the bourbon and water was empty.

Wick took a last drag and flipped the butt into the bushes planted by the side of the restaurant.

He felt like a fool sneaking around to smoke, but he'd felt like a bigger fool when Maya had almost caught him buying a pack of cigarettes from the machine. Thank the man upstairs, he was a fast improviser and there was gum in that machine. He'd finish this pack, then quit on his own. Cold turkey. He could do it.

As he approached the table, he saw Maya sitting alone sipping her wine. "Sorry you beat me back. I stepped outside with an old friend for a couple of minutes."

"No problem." She smiled.

She had a dynamite smile, warm and sincere. And she had a way of looking at a person as if he were the only soul in the world. It came, he suspected, from a maturity and inner confidence that allowed her to forget about herself and focus on other people.

They ordered dinner. He had raw oysters, fried shrimp, and a baked potato piled high with the works; she had broiled perch and a salad. Why she was on a diet, he didn't know. She had a great figure. He'd never been attracted to women who were all sharp elbows and jutting hipbones. And besides being easy on the eyes, she was a very bright lady. He found that he liked that. She snapped to things quicker than any of the women he usually dated.

She tried to bring up business once or twice, but he'd sidestepped and turned the conversation to other things. He was surprised to discover that she was a baseball fan.

"Why should that surprise you? Psychologists like baseball too. And with David in the house, I could hardly ignore it. I spent hours carpooling him to practice and rooting for his Little League team. And in high school, I never missed one of his games even though it played havoc with my schedule."

Over coffee he said, "I've got a couple of tickets to the Astros game Saturday afternoon. Why don't you come with me?"

Before she answered, she looked down at her cup and absently ran one long finger around the rim. "Wick, are you asking me for a date?"

Why lie? He grinned. "Yeah."

Her chin lifted and those lovely green eyes looked right into his. "Why?"

"The usual reasons. I'm attracted to you and I enjoy your company."

"How old are you?"

He couldn't help but grin. "Old enough."

"That's no answer."

He frowned. "I'm thirty-seven, but I can't imagine what difference my age makes. I own my own business and I have a fairly healthy bank account. I got an excellent report on my last physical; I have twenty-twenty vision and my teeth are sound. I know there are a lot of weirdos running around in this town, and I'll be happy to provide references if you like."

She smiled. "I didn't mean to insult you. I don't need references; I'm a pretty good judge of character. But, Wick, I have a grown son. Two weeks ago I turned forty."

"Two weeks ago? No kidding? What day?"

She looked startled. "August twentieth."

He leaned back in his chair and laughed. "Well, I'll be damned! What do you know about that? We have the same birthday. I knew we had a lot in common. This is great. We can go to the game and have a late celebration. I'll even have them put a candle on our hot dogs. You like hot dogs?"

*   *   *

Maya waved good-bye to Wick, who had insisted on following her home, and entered the back door of the big, rambling house in West University that she had inherited from her grandmother nine years earlier. The familiar rooms bore a faint scent like the one most people associated with academic archives, a mustiness of aging volumes and hidden dust, but here it was overlaid and tempered with years of lemon oil and lavender sachets. When she allowed it to register, the distinctive smell always reminded her of her grandmother; it reminded her of home, a safe, comfortable haven.

As soon as she'd turned on the kitchen lights, she heard Wick's sports car roar away. The sound was harsh in the sedate area of fine old homes, carefully maintained, complacent and secure in nests of English ivy and Formosa azaleas. The stately old neighborhood had been a good place to raise her son. But now the house was quiet, too quiet.

Since he'd left for college, she had missed the energy of David and his friends. The house had been very empty. Thank heaven for Chelsea. Having her vivacious sister-in-law move in had saved Maya's sanity.

She kicked off her shoes and padded to the large sunroom she'd added to the back of the house several years before. It was her favorite room. Filled with windows, plush-cushioned furniture, and plants, it had an open, airy look. She didn't turn on a lamp, instead she sank down in one of the white Haitian cotton-covered couches, propped her feet on an intricately carved banyan table, and lit a cigarette. Only the light from the kitchen cast a dim glow over a beaded Kiowa cradle cover hanging on the wall beside a collection of African tribal masks.

David was gone, and she'd entered a new phase. She had a big hole to plug. Aerobics and shopping sprees didn't do the trick. Oh, she admitted she looked better than she had in years, but the gap was still there. Chelsea was a good temporary measure, but Maya knew that Chelsea wouldn't stay forever.

When her sister-in-law insisted that Maya needed a man, she'd decided maybe she did and had tentatively put up her antennae. But was Wick McCall that man? It seemed unlikely. She lit another cigarette and blew a plume of smoke toward the windows overlooking the pool.

By the time she heard the front door slam, the ashtray was heaped with the evidence of her inner turmoil.

The light flicked on.

"What are you doing sitting here in the dark?" Chelsea, a loose-limbed blonde with a gamine cut, breezed into the room and plopped down on the sofa beside Maya.

"Thinking."

"Don't you know that thinking too much is bad for the brain? The wear and tear on the cells is murder." She leaned over and counted the butts in the ashtray. "I gather the staple didn't work."

"You gather right. I'm having it taken out tomorrow. I think I'll try the gum again. How was your hot date?"

"Lukewarm." She jumped up. "Want something to drink? I think there's some lemonade in the fridge."

"Fine."

Chelsea was back in a few minutes juggling two

glasses and a jar of peanut butter. A box of crackers was under her arm, and a knife was between her teeth. After she dumped the goodies on the coffee table, she shed her sandals and settled cross-legged on the couch.

Maya watched her smear chunky peanut butter on a cracker and pop it into her mouth. "I don't understand why you don't weigh three hundred pounds."

"Metabolism." She heaped another dollop on a cracker and ate it. "Anything exciting happen on your couch today? Discover any new phobias lurking about? Hear a confession from a secret ax murderer driven by a hatred of his mother? Meet any gorgeous men with an overactive id?"

Maya laughed. Chelsea didn't expect a serious answer. "Actually, I did meet an interesting man."

"A patient?"

"No."

The knife hovered over the peanut butter jar. "And?" Making quick circles with the knife to urge Maya on, Chelsea leaned forward. "Was he a hunk?"

"He was a hunk."

"And?" The knife circled again, faster. "Come on, give. The suspense is killing me."

Maya gave a brief rundown on her meeting and evening with Wick. "And I agreed to go to the ball game with him on Saturday. I'm wondering now if I did the right thing."

"So what's to wonder? He sounds terrific, and three years difference in your ages is no big deal. After all, you're only going to a ball game, you're not planning to marry the guy. And believe me," Chelsea said with a knowing roll of her eyes, "the younger ones have a lot more stamina. After all, you've just reached your sexual peak."

She laughed. "I think you've been reading my psychology books again."

"I read it in *Cosmo*. Tell me some more about Wick McCall."

"One big problem is that he doesn't know I smoke. When I tried to get away from him to have a secret puff or two, I felt like I was starring in an old Keystone Kops movie."

"So? You've been trying to quit. Here's your perfect motivation. There's one theory that smoking is a substitute oral gratification for not being kissed enough. Maybe he's the remedy." Chelsea grinned.

Maya raised an eyebrow. "*Cosmo* again?"

"Your psychology books. Tell me more."

"In many ways he reminds me a lot of your big brother. Oh, not so much in looks—though he's blond too—but Wick has the same sort of cocky walk and devilish attitude that Ron had. That's what scares me. I'm afraid they're too much alike."

"But why? You adored Ron, and you had a great marriage."

"Yes, for the short time we had together, but we were kids. I was devastated by his death. If it hadn't been for David, I'm not sure I would have survived losing him. Ron was my hero, and I loved him. But he thrived on excitement, wild challenges, and danger. I suspect Wick is the same kind of personality. I've changed. Now, I'm not sure I have the emotional stamina to deal with Captain Marvel."

"Maya, you've got more emotional stamina than anybody I know. And anyway, he may not be anything like Ron." She globbed another pat of peanut butter on a cracker. "What kind of business does Wick have?"

"You know, I forgot to ask. Wait." She dug into the pocket of her skirt for his business card. As she read it, she could feel the blood drain from her face. "Oh . . . my . . . Lord!"

"Maya, what's wrong?"

"Helicopters! McCall *Helicopters*, Incorporated." She shuddered. "You know how I feel about those contraptions. I can't even watch *M*A*S*H* reruns without getting the creeps. And it says right here" —she tapped her finger on the card—"that they specialize in dangerous cargoes. I should have known that Fate was playing games with me. The first interesting man I've met in ages, and he has to be a non-smoker who flies kamikaze missions."

Chelsea took a bite of her cracker, licked her fingers, and peeked at the card. "It also says they sell, charter, and lease helicopters as well as offer instructions and other services including aerial photography, pipeline checks, and tours. They probably even deliver Santa Claus to Christmas parties. And anyway, obviously Wick is the boss of McCall Helicopters. Maybe he doesn't even fly."

"He flies."

"How do you know? Did he tell you?"

"Nobody has to tell me. I know the type. He's the sort of cocky helicopter pilot who loves danger and thinks he's invincible. I'll bet a thousand dollars he personally flies the dangerous cargo."

"Maya," her sister-in-law said quietly, "Ron flew rescue missions in Vietnam. The war's been over a long time. Nobody shoots at helicopters anymore."

"I know, but it's more than that. I'm gravitating toward the same kind of man. Don't you see? It's a pattern."

"No, I don't see. And sometimes you're too analytical for your own good. You're just going to a baseball game. What's the big deal?"

Maya turned the card round and round in her fingers. "The big deal is that I'm very attracted to him."

"Aha!" Chelsea grinned. "It's about time a man cracked that shell of yours. Take advantage of it. Have a flaming affair. It's not as if you're planning a lifetime commitment to the guy. "

A lifetime commitment to someone like Wick McCall? No, certainly not, Maya told herself as she sipped her lemonade. She wanted a steady rock, not a rolling stone. But an affair? The idea hadn't occurred to her. The word affair had always had a negative connotation for her. It conjured up images of rendezvous in seedy hotels and sneaking around behind potted palms for clandestine meetings with a married lover. She almost laughed aloud. She couldn't imagine Wick sneaking around anywhere. He was a man who strode through life, cocky as a rooster and bold as brass.

Perhaps it was time she redefined "affair" and gave it some serious thought.

Three

Maya picked up the phone and buzzed her secretary. "Camilla, before you go to lunch would you please bring me a container of yogurt from the fridge?"

"Why don't I hold the yogurt, Dr. S.? I've got a feeling you're about to have a better offer."

There was a quick rap on her office door, then Wick McCall sauntered in with a long-stemmed rose in his hand. One side of his mustache was lifted by a big smile, and his eyes gleamed with waggish challenge. Her breath caught as her gaze flicked over him. He wore a loose-fitting shirt rolled up to his elbows and tucked into the waistband of tight jeans. The pale peach color and soft fabric of the shirt only emphasized his masculinity. His shoulders seemed broader; his hips, leaner; his tan, deeper. And the white-blond streaks in his hair seemed to beg her to run her fingers through the unruly strands. As he approached she felt herself go warm all over. Was it possible that he'd grown even sexier overnight? Or had her estrogen level gone berserk?

Although he smiled, the predatory look in his eyes and supple movement of his body reminded her of a stalking tiger; automatically she pushed back her chair.

"What are you doing here?" she asked.

Hanging one leg over the desk corner nearest her, he leaned forward and brushed her chin with the soft petals of the rose he held. The blossom was peach colored, too, a few shades darker than his shirt.

"I didn't want to wait until tomorrow to see you. I came to give you this." He trailed the flower along the curve of her cheek, then offered it to her. "And to take you to lunch."

She took the rose, smelled it, and smiled. "Thanks for this, but I can't go to lunch. I have scads of work to do." She waved her hand over the papers on her desk.

"You've been working all morning." He pulled her to her feet. "You need a change of scenery. I'll have you back in plenty of time for your two o'clock appointment."

She raised her eyebrows. "Has Camilla been talking again?"

He grimaced and snapped his fingers. "Shoot. That just slipped out." Flinging his arm around her shoulders, he tried to look serious. "But, tell the truth, wouldn't you rather have a great big crisp salad filled with succulent fat pink shrimp drenched in luscious creamy remoulade sauce than *yogurt*?"

She gave him a pained look. "You certainly know how to tempt a lady."

He flashed her a naughty grin. "Yes, ma'am. I do."

"I may regret this, but let's go."

Before she had time to gather her suit jacket or bag, he escorted her out the door. As they passed through the outer office, she thrust the rose into Camilla's hand. "Put this in water for me, will you?"

"Have fun," Camilla said, giving her a sly wink.

High noon on a Houston September day was rarely conducive to strolling, but, once outside, they decided to brave the heat and walk the short distance to the Galleria. They cut through Neiman Marcus to the mall and went to her favorite atrium café overlooking the indoor ice rink on the lower level. They watched the skaters while they drank cool minted tea and ate huge shrimp salads.

During their meal, Maya saw two of three young women at the next table staring at Wick and whispering to each other. The third, whose back was to them, casually glanced over her shoulder. Her eyes widened and she quickly turned around.

Maya smiled. Wick hadn't noticed his admirers. His total attention was focused on her. She liked that; it did wonders for her ego.

"What do psychologists like to do for fun, besides go to baseball games?" he asked.

"The same things that other people do. I like to watch old movies, read mysteries, swim, and do some gardening when I have time. Very ordinary things. I noticed on your business card that you have a helicopter company. Do you fly them?" Her question was casual, but she held her breath as she waited for his answer.

He nodded. "But not too much these days. I have six pilots on staff, and my business has grown so fast that I spend most of my time in the office."

Her sigh of relief was almost audible. "What about flying dangerous cargo?"

He looked amused. "The most dangerous thing we've flown lately is a prize ram to a stock show in San Antonio. He got airsick." They laughed. "Have you ever ridden in a chopper?"

"No," she said sharply, turning her attention to the skaters below. "Oh, look at that couple on the rink. There, the girl in red." She pointed to a pair dancing on the ice. "Doesn't that look like fun?"

"Do you skate?"

"I used to, but I haven't been on skates in years."

"Me neither." He peeled off money for the check and stood. "But I'm game. Let's do it."

"Do what?"

"Go skating."

"Now?" Laughing, she looked down at her slim skirt and silk blouse. "I'm hardly dressed for it."

"No problem."

Before she could convince him otherwise, he'd spirited her into a boutique a few steps away and headed for a rack. "This about your size?" When she nodded, he picked out a pair of muted green slacks and a matching cotton sweater. He grinned as he held them up against her. "I like these. They're the color of your eyes." He paid the cashier. "While you change, I'll go rent the skates. What size do you wear?"

"Seven and a half, but—"

"Meet you at the rink." He loped off while she stood shaking her head. Finally she shrugged and went to the dressing room.

When she went downstairs a few minutes later, Wick's skates were on and he held another pair in his hand.

"This is insane," she said. She couldn't believe she had bought an outfit to use during one lunch hour.

"Aw, you're going to love it." He knelt at her feet and laced up her skates. When she stood on wobbly legs, he winked up at her. "That's a good-looking outfit. Where'd you get it?"

"Some crazy man bought it for me."

He looked her up and down, then nodded smugly. "He has good taste."

He took her hand and led her onto the ice. Their first few turns around the rink were shaky, and they laughed when they almost fell twice, but soon they caught the rhythm and were gliding over the ice in unison. After a few additional rounds, they improved even more. With one firm hand at her waist and his other holding hers, Wick held her close to him, and they skimmed around the rink in great sweeping arcs, their blades perfectly synchronized.

The chill of the ice and the warmth of his body and the speed of their movement fluttering her hair made her feel deliciously alive. She laughed aloud from the sheer exhilaration of it.

He leaned close to her. "I told you you'd love it." He nuzzled her cheek, and her blades bobbled. "Whoops," he said, holding her more firmly as she regained her footing.

They grew confident and their steps became more and more elaborate until Wick tried an intricate move and they tumbled down in a heap.

"Are you hurt?" he asked as he pulled her to her feet.

She shook her head. "Only my pride." She rubbed her bottom. "I guess we're gong to have to practice once or twice more before we try out for the Olympics."

"At least." He tweaked her nose. "I'd like to keep you here all afternoon, but it's one thirty-five."

"Good heavens! Where did the time go? I've got to get back to the office."

After they removed their skates, Wick waited outside the boutique while she changed back into her work clothes. She felt great—better than great. She felt fantastic. The effects of being on ice, gliding instead of walking, lingered in her body, made her legs feel strange. A good kind of strange. She felt expanded somehow, lighter, bubbly. She was still smiling when he walked her to her office door a few minutes before two. She figured she might look a bit sappy, but she didn't care. She savored the feelings he'd sparked in her.

"I can't remember when I've had so much fun at lunch, Wick. Thank you."

He looked into her eyes, laid his hand on her cheek, and rubbed his thumb over the corner of her mouth. "Have dinner with me tonight."

"Oh, I can't," she said, genuinely disappointed. "I'm sorry. I have an important committee meeting with some colleagues. It's been planned for weeks."

His thumb ventured to the curve of her lower lip. "I can come by your house later." His voice was almost a whisper.

"I'm not sure what time the session will end. Usually these things run very late. I'll see you tomorrow."

He started to speak, then stopped and gave a slight shrug of his shoulders, as if in reluctant concession. "Noon," he said. His thumb made a final pass along the curve of her lip, and his eyes followed the movement.

Something melted inside her. At that moment she wanted nothing more than his lips warm and wet against hers. But they were standing in a public place. "I had a wonderful time, Wick. Thank you, again."

He dropped his hand and smiled. "Any time, lovely lady." He opened the door for her, and she wiggled her fingers good-bye as he left.

Her sappy smile must have still been in place when she reentered her office. Camilla raised her eyebrows. "Looks like you had a *go-od* time," the secretary said.

Maya leaned against the closed door. "Mmmmm."

"Do some shopping?"

Maya looked down at the bag in her hands. "These are my ice-skating clothes."

"Ice-skating? You went ice-skating?"

"Sure. It's a lovely way to spend lunch." She floated toward her inner office.

Saturday morning Maya sat at the breakfast table with a cigarette and a cup of coffee. Every time she took a puff from the cigarette she popped the heavy rubber band circling her wrist.

Chelsea, rumple-haired and bleary-eyed, wandered in and filled a mug from the percolator. After a couple of sips, she moved to the table, watching Maya puff, and thwack the rubber band.

"What in the world are you doing?" Chelsea asked.

"Behavioral modification using aversion therapy. The idea is that if I snap the band each time I take a puff, I'll begin to associate pain with cigarettes instead of pleasure."

"Is it working?"

Maya looked down at her reddened wrist. "I've begun to associate pain with rubber bands." She stubbed out her cigarette and tossed the rubber band into the ashtray. "I can't tell you how disgusted I feel with myself. I'm a psychologist. I should be able to lick a simple thing like nicotine."

"Don't be so hard on yourself. After all, psychologists aren't perfect."

"You know that, and I know that, but I still have to find a way to quit."

Chelsea slipped a cinnamon roll into the microwave. "I still think my kissing theory is the answer. Have you tried it yet?"

"Nope."

"Pity. What time is the hunk coming by? I want to be sure and check him out."

"About noon. But I'm not sure that I want to go. I've been thinking of calling and canceling."

"Whatever for? He sounds like a dream." Chelsea plunked the plate with the gooey roll on the table and sat down.

"He *is* a dream. My hormones almost have hysterics every time he comes within ten feet of me."

"Then what's the problem?"

"There's still this." She held up a cigarette butt. "And the helicopters. And the age difference. And—"

"And?"

Maya grabbed the cinnamon roll from Chelsea's plate and ate half of it. "And I'm not sure I'm ready for a flaming affair."

Chelsea crowed with laughter. "So you have been considering it."

"Interminably. Don't these bloodshot orbs tell the story of a restless night?"

"I vote yes."

Maya fired her a withering look. "My love life is not a matter for the ballot box." She stood. "I'm going to try to revive my eyes with cucumber slices before I have to get dressed. That is, if I decide to go to the game."

A flaming affair. Maya turned the words over and over in her mind as she dressed. She'd never thought of herself as the flaming affair type. She was a mother, a psychologist, a stable member of the community. Not a vamp. But she was also a woman who had sublimated her own sexuality for a long time. She zipped the front of her khaki jumpsuit and brushed her hair until it fell in deep waves around her shoulders.

Could she handle an affair? she wondered as she put on her makeup. She honestly didn't know. But if she was going to try it, Wick McCall was the perfect candidate. He affected her at a deep, visceral level. He oozed sensuality. And she couldn't think of a single other man that she would lose sleep over.

Of course, most of the men she knew were either married or neurotic. Too, her assumption that Wick was interested in pursuing an affair might be premature. She laughed at her reflection in the mirror. Who was she kidding? He was interested. A man didn't look at a woman the way he looked at her unless he was interested.

The doorbell rang as Maya fastened gold hoops in her ears.

"I'll get it," Chelsea yelled.

Maya stepped into Loafers and picked up her leather shoulder bag, checking to make sure she had cigarettes *and* matches.

Today, she vowed, she as going to tell Wick that she smoked. He could either like it or lump it. She was *not* going to sneak around like a juvenile hiding from the principal.

As she came down the hall she could hear Wick and Chelsea laughing. The sound surprised her for a moment. Then it occurred to her that the two of them might be better suited than Wick and she were.

He stood as Maya entered the room. He was wearing jeans, running shoes, and an Astros T-shirt. He looked very sexy. And very young. Suddenly she felt every one of her forty years.

His eyes flicked over her, then his face creased with a slow grin. "You look sensational."

"Thanks," Maya said.

Chelsea, standing behind Wick, clutched her chest and mouthed, "Wow."

Wow, indeed, Maya thought. His presence seemed to fill the room. Intimate signals from his eyes and her intense reaction to him convinced her that the attraction between them wasn't her overactive imagination. She felt the lure again, stronger this time.

"Ready?" he asked Maya, his gaze never leaving her.

She nodded and they said good-bye to Chelsea.

"I like your house," he said as they walked outside. He ran his fingers over one of the carved porch posts and looked around. "They don't build houses as solid as this anymore. Have you lived here long?"

"Most of my life. It belonged to my grandparents. Since Mom and Dad's work usually took them to remote parts of the world, I stayed with Gram during the school year until I graduated from high school. After I got my doctorate, my son and I moved back here. David needed a stable environment, and Gram's health was failing. It's a good neighborhood; most people are longtime residents and have known each other for years. I loved growing up here. There were lots of trees to climb."

He laughed and tugged an auburn curl that brushed her shoulder. "Somehow I can't picture you in pigtails and climbing trees."

"Oh, but I did. Especially those." She pointed to huge live oaks lining the avenue. Their gnarled roots cracked and buckled the sidewalks, and their limbs spread out to meet their counterparts and form a canopy across the street. "My mother was only eight or nine years old when those trees were planted. By the time I was that age, they were perfect for climbing. I used to spend hours up there, reading a book or pretending to be Wonder Woman."

"When I was eight, I always wanted to be Spider-man. I tied my dad's fishing line to my bedpost and broke my arm jumping out of the upstairs window."

"I figured you for a daredevil. I suppose you learned your lesson the hard way."

He laughed. "That I did. The next time I tried it, I used a rope. It worked fine."

"Are you still the adventurous type?"

"You bet." One corner of his mustache lifted and his eyes flashed with mischief.

She'd been afraid of that. When his hand touched the small of her back to guide her to his red Corvette, the simple contact sent ripples up her spine. Why did she have to be attracted to this utterly unsuitable man? Why couldn't he have been a nice middle-aged pediatrician who drove a Lincoln and played chess for excitement?

As they drove to the Astrodome she chewed her lip and dithered. Did she want to continue seeing him? Would she have an affair without an emotional commitment?

"Penny?"

Maya startled. "Pardon?"

"You seemed lost in deep thought."

"I was just wondering how the Astros were going to do today with their best first baseman out with injuries."

They started talking about the game and the Astros' standing in the division, and her concerns were pushed to a back corner of her mind. They parked near the stadium and followed the crowd into the air-conditioned dome that was filled with pregame noise and the smell of popcorn.

As they passed the No Smoking signs on their way to seats behind th Astros' dugout, she remembered that she hadn't yet confessed about her smoking.

Wick must have noticed the signs as well, for he said, "Now that smoking has been banned in the dome seats, we don't have to be bothered with someone else's filthy habit. Nothing's worse than sitting next to some joker puffing on a cigar or a cigarette."

She managed a feeble smile as they settled into their seats. "I know what you mean." Oh, mercy, she was getting bogged down in this mess. Now she was too embarrassed to say anything.

"I'll go get the hot dogs before the game starts. You like mustard?"

"Lots of it."

"Beer or soft drink?"

"Diet cola, please."

"You got it." He winked and patted her thigh. "I'll be right back."

She ran her hand over the place he'd patted.

Even that casual touch affected her. Why did he have to be so darned appealing? Why did her libido—successfully sublimated for so long—zero in on this man? She couldn't explain what it was about Wick McCall that made her feel so excited and alive when she was around him. Whatever it was, it was potent. And it made her nervous. She always grew anxious when her emotions strayed from her control. And when she was anxious, she wanted to smoke.

She was sorry she hadn't volunteered to get the food. She could have had a cigarette. Sighing, she tried to stem her frustration by opening the program and becoming engrossed in player bios.

The first batter took two balls and a strike before Wick returned carrying a cardboard tray. He set the tray at his feet, picked up a hot dog and handed it to her.

"Happy Birthday."

The hot dog, liberally slathered with mustard, had a small pink candle stuck in the middle of it. She laughed as he whipped a lighter from his pocket and set the candle aflame.

"Quick," he said, "make a wish and blow it out before the fire marshall throws us out on our ear."

The wish was easy.

In the top of the fourth inning, the Astros and the Braves were tied one and one. The Braves batter hit a line drive and the third-base runner broke for home. The shortstop fired the ball to the catcher as the runner slid for the plate.

"Safe!" the umpire called.

Maya, like half the stadium, jumped to her feet. "*Safe?* Are you blind?" she yelled. "You dumb dork! He was out by a mile!" Scowling, she turned to Wick and hit him on the knee. "Don't just sit there laughing at me. Didn't you see he was out? *Do* something."

He stood, put his arms around her, and gave her a great smacking kiss. "You're dynamite when you're mad. Did you get thrown out of many Little League games?"

A flush crawled up her throat, and she sunk back down into her seat. "I tend to get carried away at baseball games. Did I embarrass you?"

"Hell, no. I'll get you a megaphone if you want one." Chuckling, he sat beside her and laced her fingers with his.

"He was out," she muttered.

"Damn right he was." He squeezed her fingers.

By the bottom of the seventh inning, the Astros were leading four to three, and Maya had consumed two hot dogs and a bag of popcorn. Shells from three packages of peanuts littered the floor at her feet. She was too mortified to ask Wick to get her anything else to eat—though she had to admit he'd been a good sport about it, insisting on going to the concession stand himself instead of waiting for a vendor to come by.

He stretched his arm across the back of her seat, and his thumb absently stroked her shoulder. Her stomach contracted. His knee brushed hers and she jumped. She tried deep breathing; she dug an old butterscotch candy from the bottom of her purse and sucked on it. It didn't help. She had to have a cigarette.

Mumbling an excuse about going to the ladies' room, she climbed over a dozen pair of feet and practically ran to a smoking area. It was easy to spot. Several people crowded around a big ashtray, and the air around them was hazy. The smell drew her like a homing signal.

She quickly lit up and inhaled. She took another puff and another, damning herself in between each one for being such a wimpy weakling. Soon she was either going to have to find a way to quit or she was going to have to accept the fact that she was a smoker forever. And tell Wick.

A well-dressed woman standing beside her flicked ashes into the receptacle and smiled at Maya. "We smokers have become pariahs nowadays, haven't we?"

Maya returned her smile. "Seems that way."

"Nobody seems sympathetic to our plight. My children are always after me to quit, but I haven't been too successful."

"It can be very difficult."

Diamonds on the woman's fingers flashed as she took another puff and blew the smoke upward. Maya pasted a smile on her face, murmured something sympathetic, and hightailed it to the ladies' room. She rinsed her mouth and scrubbed her hands, then did it all over again before she went back to her seat.

Wick smiled as she slipped in beside him. "I missed you."

"Long lines," she mumbled.

He casually laid his hand on her thigh as he leaned over to catch her up on the game. Her heart did a flip-flop, and it was difficult to concentrate on his words as the tips of his fingers lightly stroked her leg. Strange that such a simple touch should affect her so, but it did. She promised herself that by the time the afternoon was over, she would decide if she wanted to pursue any kind of relationship with him.

Why did life have to be so complicated?

As she tried to sort out the pros and cons, she

became more and more anxious. And, as usual, the more anxious she became, the more she wanted the comfort of a cigarette. Of all times for such a fluke, the game went to thirteen innings. With a couple of trips to the "ladies' room" and four more bags of peanuts, she endured.

By the time Glenn Davis hit a home run in the bottom of the thirteenth, she had decided to either tell Wick she smoked and have a flaming affair or end the whole thing with a cool brush-off when he took her home.

The problem was that she vacillated between the two decisions from one second to the next. Each option had a long mental list of supporting arguments.

On the way home Wick said, "Want to go someplace for dinner?"

Sucking on her fifth wintergreen breath mint, she gave him a pained look. "Are you kidding? I'm up to my eyes in peanuts. I probably won't eat again until next Tuesday."

The deep resonance of his laughter filled the car. "I had several bags myself. Why is it that peanuts always taste better at the ballpark?"

By the time he walked her to the door, she'd made her decision. The brush-off. Definitely the brush-off. As much as she enjoyed being with him, she was going to call this thing to a ha't before she became too deeply involved. She refused to submit herself to any more anguish. He was too young, too sexy, too distracting, too wrong.

She unlocked the door and turned to him. She'd opened her mouth to tell him good night and good-bye when the look in his eyes cut off the words.

Desire radiated from their golden depths, and

his hand reached out to cup her cheek. His fingers extended into the hairline at the side of her neck and gently massaged. His gaze went from her eyes to her lips and his mouth slowly lowered toward hers. The first touch was soft, a tentative teasing and testing.

She considered pulling away. She really did. But the warmth generated by his closeness and the delicious feel of his lips against hers made her linger.

When she sighed softly, his touch changed. His arms went around her and pulled her against him. He kissed her like she'd never been kissed before. Her mind went weak and her knees followed suit; her arms automatically clung to him. There was nothing tentative or hesitant about the lips moving over hers, about the tongue that demanded entrance to taste and explore.

He groaned and pulled away. "I've been wanting to do that since the first time I saw you. It's even better than I'd imagined. Woman, you set me on fire."

He kissed her again and the last vestiges of reason vanished. Her senses ran amok. Her hormones went wild. Her tongue slid under his and he moaned. Her hands rubbed down the length of his back to his hips and pulled him against her. A low sound reverberated deep within his throat.

Drawing away slightly so that his mouth was only millimeters from hers, he said, "Let's go inside before we give the neighbors a show they're not likely to forget."

She sucked in a shuddering breath, then another. "No. You'd better go." She pushed against his chest. "Things are moving too fast for me; I can't seem to think clearly."

He touched his forehead to hers. "I know the feeling." He gave her a quick kiss. "I'll call you tomorrow."

"Tomorrow."

She didn't remember until much later that she hadn't planned to see him again.

That night, after Chelsea left with another potential hot date, Maya sat at the kitchen table catching up on paperwork. Or trying to. Her mind kept wandering off, replaying her afternoon with Wick.

A pecking on the glass of the kitchen door drew her attention, and she peeked through the yellow curtains. Recognizing the spare, slightly stooped figure of her next-door neighbor, she smiled as she opened the door to the elderly man.

"I'm looking for John Keats. That rascal isn't hiding out over here, is he?"

"No, 'Fessor," she said, using the comfortable name she'd called Professor Charles Malcolm Newberry since she was a toddler. "Would you like me to help you look for him?"

John Keats was an independent Abyssinian cat who sometimes liked to escape the comfort and security of his home and prowl the back alleys looking for a little excitement.

"No, no, I don't suspect it would do any good to search for the scamp. He'll come home when it suits his purpose."

"He always does. I wouldn't worry about him." She smiled at the retired professor of English literature who preferred ascots to neckties and was wearing a wine-colored one at the throat of his starched white collar. "Would you come in and join me for a cup of tea?"

His wrinkled face perked up. "I wouldn't say no to a nice cup of chamomile."

While she put the kettle on, the white-haired gentleman settled into his customary seat in the breakfast nook. The professor and Walter Chapman, his companion for over forty years, had been surrogate grandfathers for her when she was growing up. 'Fessor and Chappy had repaired her doll buggies and taught her to ride her first two-wheeled bike. They'd performed a similar role for David. Chappy had died last year. She missed him.

When the tea was brewed, she brought the china service to the table to pour. They sipped for a moment in companionable silence.

"The house is very quiet these days with David gone," he said.

"Yes, it is. There always used to be a crowd here. I was often afraid the neighbors would complain about the loud music and horseplay of all his friends."

"Oh, no. Walter and I loved to hear the laughter and bustle of the young people. Why, once Walter said—" He stopped and his soft blue eyes glazed over for a moment.

Maya laid her hand over his. "You miss Chappy very much, don't you?"

He set down his cup and patted the hand that comforted his. "That I do, my dear. That I do. It gets very lonely rattling around that big house with nothing but a cantankerous cat for company. That's why I'm concerned about you. I'm an old man, but you're young yet." He patted her hand again and leaned closer. "Now I don't want you to think I'm a nosy old busybody but, when I was out vacuuming my car earlier, I could hardly help but notice that a gentleman in a sporty red automobile brought you home. Is it too much to hope that you have a new beau?"

"He was just a man I've seen a few times. We went to a baseball game. I don't think it's going to be anything serious. I'm not sure that I'll be seeing him again."

The old man's face fell. "Oh, I had hoped—" He sighed.

" 'Fessor, he's younger than I am."

"Piffle, my dear. Age means nothing. Why Robert Browning was several years younger than Elizabeth, and theirs was one of the great love affairs of the ages."

Maya laughed. "Wick McCall is hardly a Robert Browning."

"Do you find Mr. McCall attractive?"

She nodded.

"Does he seem to return your interest?"

She nodded.

"Does he treat you kindly and considerately?"

She nodded again.

He patted her hand. "Then allow the relationship a bit of time to mature." He smiled. "One never knows what might develop."

Four

Maya was cleaning her closet and chewing hard on a piece of nicotine gum when the doorbell rang. She was barefoot and dressed in an old pair of shorts and one of David's cast-off T-shirts.

"Rats!" She dumped a load of blouses on her bed and tucked a stray strand of hair into the rubber band holding the rest of it atop her head.

The doorbell rang again. Chelsea was at the law library studying for a course in contracts, and, since Maya wasn't expecting anyone, she considered not answering it. But she'd never been the type of person who could ignore telephones and doorbells. Her innate curiosity always won.

She opened the door to find Wick leaning one hand against the frame and frowning. The frown changed to a smile when he saw her.

"I was afraid you weren't home," he said. "I tried to call, but your number is unlisted."

Mortified that he'd found her looking her worst, she almost groaned. She should have told her curiosity to get lost. "What are you doing here?" she blurted out.

He laughed. "I thought you might like to go bike riding."

"I'm sorry. I'm in the middle of cleaning my closet."

"Is that like washing your hair?"

She couldn't prevent a chuckle. "I really *am* cleaning my closet."

"It's too nice a day to be cooped up inside. Put on some jeans and let's go for a ride. Though it's a shame," he said, his eyes traveling over her, "to cover beautiful legs like those."

She shifted uncomfortably, but there was nowhere to hide. "I don't think so, but thank you."

"Aw, come on. You can clean your closet later. I'll even buy you lunch." His gold eyes taunted and his mustache curved upward with a beguiling grin.

She hesitated. If she had any sense at all, she would tell him no and close the door. But when she was around Wick, her good sense seemed to go into limbo. All she could think about was how good he looked in his jeans and blue polo shirt, how absolutely devastatingly handsome he was, how he reminded her of pomegranates and leather and wind in her hair.

She frowned as an idea tweaked the edge of her preoccupation. It struck her as strange that Wick wanted to go bike riding. Somehow she couldn't picture him tooling a ten-speed around the neighborhood.

She cocked her head. "What kind of bike do you have?"

He grinned. "A Harley."

"*Harley?* As in motorcycle?"

He nodded and glanced over his shoulder to the curb in front. She stared at the big machine that sat there, black and menacing, with enough chrome for two Cadillacs and a Rolls-Royce.

"You expect *me* to go riding on that thing? I've never ridden a motorcycle in my life."

"All you have to do is hang on. I'll do the rest." One corner of his mouth lifted in a taunting smile. His hand cupped the side of her cheek, and his index finger toyed with her earlobe. She tensed, and he smiled and said softly, "You'll be safe with me. I promise."

"Will I, Wick? Will I be safe with you?"

"I'm no green kid. I know what I'm doing." His eyes were on her mouth, and his thumb brushed the curve of her lower lip. His voice was a seductive whisper. "Trust me. You'll love it."

Maya clutched Wick's waist as they roared down the street. Why had she ever agreed to this? Her behavior was pathological. Certifiable. Yet, here she was, dressed in jeans, an old pullover, and a helmet, clinging for dear life while he zipped around like a madman.

When they stopped for a traffic light, Wick flipped up the smoked visor of his helmet, looked over his shoulder at her, and grinned.

"Relax, sweetheart." He patted one of her hands that gripped his midsection. "Not that I don't enjoy you hanging on to me, but you're cutting off the circulation."

She loosened her hold, marginally. "I don't know how I ever let you talk me into this."

He laughed. "Here we go." He flipped the visor down and with a *varoom, varoom,* they sped away.

She squeezed her lids shut and hung on. When, a few minutes later, she found she was still alive, she opened her eyes again. They were on the freeway. Thankfully, there was very little traffic. She could feel her heart pounding against her chest and was sure he could feel it as well since her breasts were flattened against his back.

As the big machine roared down the highway without mishap, she gradually began to ease her death grip. In fact, she was surprised to discover that riding on the motorcycle with the wind whipping past was a pleasant experience. More than pleasant. She felt remarkably exhilarated and unrestrained. Truthfully, she found that she liked it.

With her adrenaline under control, she began to be aware of other things—the feel of his taut abdomen beneath her fingers, the warmth of his back against her breasts, the breadth of his shoulders. The insides of her thighs were pressed close to his hips and their juncture rested just above his belt. The vibrations of the powerful machine turned their proximity into a sensual maelstrom.

She wiggled and squirmed, trying to ease back in the chrome-studded passenger seat, but she couldn't move much unless she let go of him, and she wasn't about to do that.

When she fidgeted again, his shoulders started shaking. The devil was laughing! She pinched him, and he patted her hand. She wiggled some more and tried to think of other things. But her mind slid back to the man astride the Harley.

Her stomach contracted and her chest tightened. A low ache spread through her body and heated her skin. Denying its source, she focused her thoughts on patients she would see the next day, grocery lists, Carl Jung's theory of the collective unconscious. But Jung made her think of Freud, and Freud made her think of sex, and she was right back where she started.

Half an hour later they turned off the highway onto a two-lane asphalt road and then onto another. Wick slowed as they wound around a deserted stretch shaded by tall trees rippled by September breezes. After a mile or so, he turned onto a sandy lane, and her teeth jarred as they bumped across a cattle guard.

Rolling to a stop where a thicket of pines edged a field, he set the stand and helped her off. They removed their helmets and she finger combed her hair, grateful there was some distance between them at last.

"How'd you like your first motorcycle ride?"

"It wasn't as bad as I thought it might be."

He gave her a teasing wink. "Aw, come on, admit it. You might have been a little nervous at first, but you liked riding my hawg, didn't you? I told you I knew what I was doing."

His gaze flicked over her and she looked away. Yes, he knew what he was doing. He'd used that damned motorcycle as foreplay. This whole situation was fraught with sexual symbolism and double entendres. All her thoughts of having a flaming affair with him disappeared. She wasn't ready for an affair with someone she'd met only a few days ago.

She might never be ready.

Being around Wick made her feel ill at ease, reminded her that she'd been out of the dating and mating game so long that she didn't know the rules anymore. She didn't know how to act, and she didn't like the feeling. She preferred to be in control of situations or, at least, to be able to conduct herself with aplomb. He seemed to delight in throwing her off-guard.

She turned her attention to their surroundings.

Golden wild flowers bobbed their brown-centered heads in the grassy field, and wind sighed through the stand of pines in cool invitation. Ordinarily she would have enjoyed the peace, solitude, and beauty of the spot. Now it only made her nervous. Miles from the city and with not another soul in sight, this was the perfect spot for seduction.

"Where are we?" She glanced at Wick, who was watching her with a knowing grin on his face. She could have strangled him.

"The land belongs to my oldest sister, Sara, and her husband, Joe."

"Do they live on the property?"

He shook his head. "Nobody lives here. Joe plans to become a gentleman farmer when he retires from his law practice in Houston." He laughed. "Sara has told him he'd better get a dog to keep him warm, because she doesn't plan to move to the country."

Maya managed a smile. The smile faded when she saw Wick pull a ground cloth from one of the Harley's saddlebags. He walked to a spot under the trees, and she frowned when he spread the cloth over a thick layer of pine needles. Surely he didn't think she was game for a quick tumble in the woods?

"And what's *that* for?" she asked.

One eyebrow went up, one side of his mouth lifted, and he hung his thumbs in the waistband of his jeans. "What do you think it's for?"

"I don't know. Hadn't we better be getting back?"

"Not yet. I promised you lunch. I thought you might enjoy a picnic out here."

"Oh."

He lifted her chin and looked into her eyes. "Relax, babe. I didn't plan on anything more than a quiet picnic in the country, some conversation, maybe a kiss or two if you're willing. Are you afraid of me?"

"Of course not. A little anxious, maybe. Even though I'm forty years old, I haven't had a relationship with a man in a long time. I don't quite know how to behave."

"You're doing fine." He dropped a kiss on her nose. "We'll take it slow and easy. You set the pace." He took her hand. "Let's eat. I'm starving."

They unpacked the food stowed in his saddle-bags and carried it to the ground cloth. From a paper sack Wick took a large submarine sandwich and handed it to her. "A loaf of bread." He pulled a bottle of champagne from an insulated sleeve. "A jug of wine." He grinned as he emptied the bag. "Potato salad, paper plates, and thou."

She laughed as he bent and kissed her hand. "You're a nut."

Devilment danced in his eyes. "Yes, ma'am." He snapped his fingers. "I forgot something."

"Napkins? Forks?"

"They're in the sack. I'll be right back."

While Maya divided the huge sandwich and potato salad onto paper plates, Wick disappeared for a moment. When he returned, he had a fistful of golden wild flowers. He held them out to her. "For you, m'lady."

She dipped her head as she took them. "Thank you, kind sir." she laid them in the middle of the cloth, and he set about opening the champagne. "I don't think I've ever had champagne on a picnic before."

He grinned. "Good. I want this to be special."

He untwisted the wires and began easing out the cork with his thumbs. With a loud pop the cork shot up in a high arc and hit a tree twenty feet away. Wine gushed from the bottle and spewed over them. Laughing, she grabbed plastic glasses and held them under the foamy geyser.

Looking sheepish, he licked wine from his hands. "I don't think the champagne rode too well."

She chuckled. "I can empathize."

He laughed and clicked his glass against hers. "To better rides."

His tone was low and blatantly suggestive. Even though her heartbeat accelerated, she ignored his remark.

After they'd finished lunch and stowed the trash in the bag, Wick poured the last of the champagne in their glasses. Maya leaned against a pine tree and sipped hers while he stretched out on his side. She felt relaxed, sated.

"That was wonderful," she said. "I can't remember when I was last on a picnic."

"Camilla says you work too hard. You need to get out more, have a little fun."

"I've been promising myself that I would, yet I never seem to find the time. You run a business; you know how it is."

He shook his head and picked up several stems of the flowers lying on the cloth. "I run a business; it doesn't run me. Life is to be enjoyed."

She watched, surprised, as he began weaving the flowers together. His movements were skillful, almost automatic, as if he'd had hours of practice in the simple pastime. He seemed an unlikely man to know how to fashion daisy chains, she thought, then chided herself for her sexist attitude. She really didn't know much about him.

"You do that very well," she said.

He chuckled as he picked up more flowers. "I think I mentioned that I have three older sisters. They taught me all sorts of things. I'm pretty good with hair bows and sashes too. It comes in handy when I baby-sit with Kathy's little girls."

"Kathy? One of your sisters?"

"My niece. She's Sara and Joe's older daughter. Beth, their younger, is in college."

"Do all your sisters live in the area?"

"No, Penny and her family live in Dallas, and Deanna and her daughter live in Atlanta." He continued weaving as he told her anecdotes about being the only boy in a family of girls.

She took a sip of wine. "I envy you. As an only child, I always wanted a big family."

"You've been a widow for a long time. Why haven't you married again?"

She shrugged. "The usual answer, I suppose. I didn't find the right person. What about you?"

"In my younger days I wasn't looking. I planned to go to Vietnam as soon as I finished college, but by the time I graduated, the war was over. I missed it by only a couple of months. I did a hitch in the marines anyway, but I didn't like military life. I liked flying the hot spots, but most of the time it was too boring, too confining. After I got out, I still wasn't ready to settle down. I went to work flying choppers for an oil company and raised a little hell in Singapore for a couple years. That got boring, too, and I decided to move on.

"Then I knocked around Florida for a while. A buddy of mine had a salvage boat and big plans for finding sunken treasure in the Caribbean. Bingo talked me into going partners with him. We spent a year and a half diving and trying to find it."

She laughed. "A futile search, right?"

"Uh-uh. We found it. Oh, we didn't make as big a haul as Fisher, but it was big enough. By that time I was tired of bumming around and living out of a duffel bag, so I decided to settle in Houston, put down some roots, and start a business. I can still pick up and go adventuring when the mood strikes me, but I've got a home base."

She watched him weave two ends of the flower chain together into a crown. "And you never met that special woman?"

He moved over and placed the circlet on her head. "No, not until now."

Her breath caught and she went still. Before she could say anything, his lips moved over hers. They were sun warm, petal soft, and tasted of champagne. She ached to deepen the kiss, but his mouth withdrew and his mustache tickled a sensual trail to her ear.

"You have the softest skin," he whispered. He nipped her earlobe and drew a line along her jaw with the tip of his tongue.

Her eyes closed and her fingers tightened around the glass she held as she savored the sensations he aroused. She was disappointed when he moved away to stretch out and settle his head in her lap.

"Nice pillow," he murmured and his lids drifted shut.

She gulped the last of her wine, trying to quench the fire he had ignited. It didn't work.

"I'm not much of an adventurer," she mused aloud.

"Somehow I don't believe that." Eyes still closed, he nestled his head more comfortably in her lap.

* * *

Wick pretended to doze, though it would have taken a better man than he was to sleep through what he was feeling. If he'd followed his impulse, he'd have Maya stripped naked and moaning by now. He wasn't a psychologist, but he'd figured that she was a lady who needed special handling or she'd retreat behind that professional aloofness.

He knew that deep inside her was a tremendous capacity for passion. He could almost feel the rumbling. He planned to take things slowly, tease that fire to the surface, and be around when it burst loose. When they made love for the first time, it was going to set off more fireworks than a Chinese New Year.

As it did every time he closed his eyes and thought of Maya, the image of the two of them on the beach came to him. He almost groaned aloud.

He hadn't had one all day, but now he was dying for a cigarette.

As they rounded the corner of her street, Maya saw Chelsea in the front yard watering the budding chrysanthemums and talking to 'Fessor. The gamine-faced blonde waved when they pulled up on Wick's motorcycle, turned off the hose, and walked to the curb. The professor, dressed in a safari outfit with a red ascot, trailed Chelsea.

Maya climbed off the motorcycle and introduced her neighbor. Wick, who stood astride the machine, thumbed up his visor and shook hands with the old gentleman.

"Been out for a ride, have you?" 'Fessor's perusal took in the big black cycle and its riders. There was a definite twinkle in his eyes. "I fancied one of these contraptions in my younger days. Quite a machine you have there, Mr. McCall."

"Um, yes, nice Harley," Chelsea said. Her eyes obviously admired both man and motorcycle. "I always wanted one, but I figured it would be too much for me to handle."

My feelings exactly, Maya thought. She took off the helmet and shook her hair. "I'm sure Wick would give you a ride. Wouldn't you, Wick?"

He hesitated a moment. "Sure. Want to try it, Dr. Newberry?"

'Fessor laughed. "Oh, no, not me, young man. My bones are too brittle for such high jinks. But I thank you for the compliment."

"Chelsea?" Maya asked.

"I'd love it."

"Hop on." Wick flipped his visor down.

The two women changed places and Maya could hear Chelsea's squeals of delighted laughter as the motorcycle roared away. She watched them go with mixed emotions. One irrational part of her resented her place being usurped even though she'd suggested the idea; a more logical part of her knew that Wick and Chelsea would be a good match.

"Seems like a nice young fellow," 'Fessor said.

"Yes, he is. And *young* is the operative word." She turned to her companion. "I think Wick and Chelsea would be better suited than he and I would, don't you?"

"What I think is of little consequence. The appropriate question is what does your young man think of the notion?"

She shrugged.

He cleared his throat in a most telling comment. "Well, John Keats is hiding again. It's a shame, since I'm off to the river house for a few days to commune with nature. You'd think the rascal would love an opportunity to chase around in the woods and dine on fresh-caught fish, but I suppose he's a city cat."

There was a suspicious rattling in the shrubbery beside the front porch, and John Keats came trotting toward them. They laughed as the purring tom wound around the professor's legs.

"Got your attention, did I, puss?" He bent to stroke the cat's head.

Maya offered to collect mail and newspapers and watch his house while he was gone. When man and cat left, she went back inside, her thoughts turning again to Wick and Chelsea. Yes, she told herself, those two were much better suited. She'd give some thought to promoting a relationship between them.

Someone knocked on her bedroom door. "Maya, are you in there?"

It as Wick! She hadn't expected them back so soon. She stubbed out her cigarette and made a dash for the bathroom. Grabbing a bottle of the strongest mouthwash she could find, she took a swig and swished it in her mouth.

He banged on the door again. "Maya!"

Making a face at the vile medicinal taste, she shuddered and spit it out. "Just a minute!"

She spritzed herself with Passion and ran around her bedroom spraying room deodorizer. Spying the cigarette butt, she grabbed the ashtray and ran to clean it and flush the evidence down the toilet.

At the door she took a deep breath. Then she turned the knob and stepped out, closing it quickly behind her. Looking up at Wick, she raised her eyebrows and said, quite calmly, "Yes?"

He laid his forearms on her shoulders and smiled. "Mmmm, you smell good."

"It's Passion."

He didn't say a word, but his slow, lascivious grin could have filled an encyclopedia.

"It's perfume. Passion is the name of a perfume. What do you want?" she asked, more sharply than she intended.

If he noticed her tone, he ignored it. "You didn't tell me good-bye."

"I'm sorry, Wick. I really did enjoy our picnic. Thank you very much. I'll walk you to the door."

He didn't move. "Chelsea invited me to stay and go for a swim. She said I could borrow a suit from David's room. That is, if you don't mind my staying."

A strange feeling gripped her heart. "No, I don't mind at all. His room is at the end of the hall. The suits should be in the bottom drawer of his chest."

He grinned. "Great. Change and I'll meet you at the pool."

"Oh, I can't go swimming. You and Chelsea go ahead. I have to finish my closet."

He reached for the doorknob to her room. "I'll help. Then we can both go. I'm fantastic with closets. I—"

"—have three sisters," they said at the same time.

"Wick, I appreciate your offer, but cleaning a closet is a very . . ." She paused, searching for an appropriate word.

"Intimate?" He looked amused.

Her chin lifted. "I was going to say 'personal thing.' But thank you anyway. You and Chelsea run along and enjoy yourselves. I'll be out later."

He frowned and looked pensive, but he didn't argue. "Later." He gave her a quick kiss.

Maya went back in her bedroom and smoked a cigarette before she tackled sorting her blouses. Maybe Wick and Chelsea would get along so well that she could stop worrying about having a flaming affair with him. Certainly he and her sister-in-law seemed well suited. They were both young and adventuresome. Yes, that was a wonderful idea. He and Chelsea could have a romance, and her life could get back to normal.

She couldn't imagine why the splashing sounds and the laughter from the pool bothered her so, but she smoked another cigarette while she rearranged her shoes.

Hoping Wick would go home and she wouldn't have to deal with him anymore, Maya stayed in her room for another half hour. But when she lifted a slat and peered through the miniblinds at the pool, he was still there. Chelsea was sunbathing on the deck, and he was stretched out on a chaise with a can of beer.

He turned his head and winked directly at her. *Damn!* The slat clicked back into place as she jerked her finger away, embarrassed to have been caught peeking. The man must have radar. And subtlety was lost on him. Why didn't he leave?

Refusing to play his game and refusing to stay a prisoner in her own house, she marched out the front door, picked up the hose, and began watering the chrysanthemums.

"What are you doing?"

She startled at the sound of the deep voice behind her and almost sprayed her foot. "Watering the flowers." She kept her attention on the plants.

"Chelsea watered them earlier, remember?"

Feeling like a nincompoop again, she released the trigger on the hose and tossed it down. She stiffened her back and raised her chin, determined that he not see how ruffled she as. "Chrysanthemums need lots of water."

He chuckled and she turned to face him. Her composure fled.

She'd seen him in the bathing suit earlier, but it had been just a glimpse. It hadn't prepared her for the sun-bronzed reality standing before her. The man was gorgeous. His chest was smooth and well muscled; his corded abdomen looked rock hard without, as far as she could tell, any particular effort to keep it sucked in. His thighs strained at the legs of David's old blue suit, and his calves curved in a most enticing way.

When her gaze traveled up the length of his body to meet his eyes, they were crinkled with amusement. She realized she'd been gaping.

Before he could say something as gauche as the "Like what you see?" she knew was eminent, she lifted her nose and forced her face into a bland expression. "Nice tan."

He threw back his head and laughed.

She was mortified. He wasn't fooled for a minute. "Wick, thank you so much for the motorcycle ride and the picnic. I had a very nice time." She stuck out her hand. "Good-bye."

Looking amused, he took her hand and drew her close. "Am I supposed to leave now? Without even getting my clothes?"

She glanced at his bare chest. "Of course not. Feel free to change in David's room. Just hang the trunks over the shower rod."

A few minutes later Maya was in the kitchen fixing herself an iced tea when Wick found her. Coming up behind her, he wrapped both arms around her waist and nuzzled the side of her neck. She almost dropped the glass.

"Mmmmm, I like that Passion," he said.

"I'll give you the bottle." She squirmed out of his hold. Getting rid of him wasn't going to be as easy as she thought.

He laughed. "I'll be back about seven to take you to dinner."

Irritated, she said, "You're certainly taking a lot for granted. I already have other plans tonight."

"Yes, I know. You promised Chelsea that you'd go with her to the new Italian restaurant on the Southwest Freeway." He grinned. "I'm taking her place."

"I have a better idea. You take Chelsea, and I can stay home and catch up on some professional reading."

"Uh-uh. If you don't go, I don't go."

"But you and Chelsea are much better suited than—"

He touched his fingers to her lips to halt the words. "I thought that might be your tactic. Maya, your sister-in-law doesn't turn me on. You do."

"But—"

This time he used his mouth to quiet her with a slow kiss that made her forget her argument.

Wick lay naked in a tangle of sheets and stared at the ceiling fan above his bed. He couldn't sleep. All he could do was think of Maya. He'd been unable to enjoy his fettuccine at dinner he'd been so busy watching her, wanting her. He didn't know how a woman could have burrowed under his skin so quickly or so thoroughly, but she had. He liked everything about her. Her sultry voice and throaty laughter echoed in his head. Her exotic face and lush body were stamped in his brain.

He didn't want to be here alone in his bed; he wanted to be with her. Even if all they did was talk, he wanted to hear her voice. He wanted to watch her smile in that slow way that lit her eyes and made his chest swell.

He reached for the phone, but the red numbers on his digital clock stopped him, and he flopped back against his pillow. He couldn't call her at two o'clock in the morning.

A smoke. He needed a smoke.

Flinging the cover aside, he got up and walked to the dresser. There were two left in the pack. He felt like a sneak hiding his habit from Maya. When these two were gone, that was it. He would quit.

He lit the cigarette, took a deep drag, and walked out onto the deck. Leaning on the banister, he looked up at the full moon, down at its reflection on the pool two floors below, took a deep drag, and thought about her some more.

No woman had ever gotten to him the way that she had. He wasn't exactly sure what it was about her, but it was something potent. It was more than having the hots for her—though, Lord knows, he did. She grabbed him somewhere deep inside. Maybe it was her openness, her caring, her basic optimism that he found so attractive. Or maybe it was that special way she had of listening and *hearing*. Or the way they could laugh together.

He liked the sound of her voice and the special way she smiled. Just being around Maya made him feel good. He had a hunch that she might be the one who could fill the empty, lonely spot that had plagued him for the last couple of years.

The thought surprised him. He'd never seriously considered a long-term relationship with anyone. His feet were too itchy. He liked the freedom to pick up and go when the urge struck him. He liked living on the edge and not having to account to anyone if he wanted to risk his neck. The responsibility of a wife and kids had always turned him off. He still wasn't certain about kids. But a special lady of his own . . . now that was worth considering.

Could he make it with someone like Maya over the long haul? It was too early in the game to call. On the surface they seemed very different, but he suspected that underneath her polished exterior was a woman with a passion for living and loving that could match his. That red hair was a dead giveaway.

Five

Maya sat at her desk making notes on the session that had just concluded. The patient, in for her third visit, was a co-dependent wife of an alcoholic, clinically depressed, and with a history of childhood sexual abuse. Maya had just made the final notation in her file when Camilla came in with correspondence needing signature.

"You look beat. Heavy session?" Camilla asked.

She blew out a puff of air and nodded. "Very heavy."

"Well, that's your last patient of the day," Camilla said. "Mrs. Wright canceled her three o'clock and rescheduled for next Tuesday, and Charlie Cossum's mother called and said he has the chicken pox. Why don't you knock off early and go buy yourself a new dress for your date with your main man?"

Maya narrowed her eyes at her secretary. "And just how did you know I have a date with Wick?"

"Oh," she said with a smug bobble of her head, "I have my ways. And even if I didn't, it doesn't take Sherlock Holmes to figure out that he wouldn't let a Friday night pass. With him sending flowers by the truckload and calling every day for the last couple of weeks, I figure things must be heating up pretty good."

"Camilla!"

"Well, you've been seeing an awful lot of him and *something's* put a bloom in your cheeks. And I noticed you only sneaked off to the broom closet four times today."

"Camilla!"

"You think I don't know when you've been in that broom closet? Humph!"

"I'm trying, Camilla. I'm really trying."

The secretary's face softened. "I know you are. And I know how much stress you're under with all these patients' problems. Beats me how you hold up under it. I won't say another word about your sneaking out."

Maya sighed. "I realize that my practice has become too much for one person to handle. I've decided to start interviewing for a partner next week. And I know I need to quit smoking, but I've tried everything I know how to do—at least twice. Nothing seems to work."

"I saw something on TV the other night—"

"I tried it six months ago. Nineteen ninety-five down the drain. I suppose I need to attack my problem with a total modality program or maroon myself on a desert island"

"One of these days, something will work. In the meantime, I'll stay off your back." She grinned. "At least your smoking doesn't seem to put off Wick McCall. Now you get your purse and go buy that dress." Camilla gathered up the papers and left.

Maya touched one of the Fiji mums in the arrangement on her desk. They were from Wick. She hadn't been able to discourage his pursuit, and his constant presence had worn down her resistance. Not that it was all that difficult for him to do. He was, after all, a very charming man. And sexy as the dickens. He made her laugh, and she enjoyed spending time with him. Having a man in her life, even temporarily, was nice. She'd finally decided to go with the flow and see where it led.

While it was true that Wick's and her relationship was heating up, Camilla's reasoning had one major flaw. She still hadn't found the right time —no, face it, she hadn't had the nerve—to tell Wick that she smoked. Her own hypocrisy and deceit began to rise up like a specter to mock her. Before it got a toehold and totally depressed her, she grabbed her purse and rushed out.

Tonight, she promised herself. She'd tell him tonight. In the meantime, she'd forget that cigarettes existed.

She wandered through Neiman until the perfect dress caught her eye. A two-piece crepe, the V-neck top had cap sleeves and a wrap front that draped softly over the hips and was caught at the waist with a big buckle. And the color was perfect for her. The straight skirt was black, and the blouse an exotic print in black and a rich tobacco —oh, no, there was that word again.

Snatching the hanger from the rack, she charged into the dressing room.

The dress was a perfect fit. It was made for seduction. And she was more than ready for Wick's and her relationship to move in that direction. In fact, she'd been surprised that he hadn't pushed things. Oh, there had been several steamy kisses, but he'd always left her at the door. Somehow that surprised her. He seemed the type to be a fast mover. Was it because he was waiting for her to set the pace? Or was it because Chelsea was in the house?

She smiled. Chelsea had left for an assignment in Dallas that morning. She wouldn't be back until Sunday. This was the perfect time for her flaming affair to begin.

Wick sat at his desk doing paperwork. He hated shuffling papers, but that was one of the drawbacks of being the boss. When the stack in the out basket was piled high, he was disgusted to discover that he had a cigarette in his hand and the ashtray was full of butts.

Damn! He'd done pretty well there for a while. But his bad habit had crept back up on him. And he knew why. Maya.

Not an hour of the day went by that he didn't think of her. Hell, even his dreams were full of her. He wanted her, ached for her. But for the past weeks, he'd held back, biding his time until he sensed she was ready to take things a step further. He knew that if he rushed her, she'd end their relationship before it got off the ground. Patience had never been his strong suit, and sometimes he wondered if she was worth the wear and tear on his peace of mind—not to mention his lungs.

Yes, he thought, she was worth it. He made a face at the cigarette smoldering between his fingers and ground it out. If Maya ever found out that he was still hooked by the damned things, he'd be dead in the water. Reaffirming that his smoking days were over, he tossed the rest of the pack in the trash and left the office.

He had a special evening planned. Dinner and dancing at the Shane Rooftop, then a moonlight flight to Kemah and his place on the Gulf.

Maya fumbled the back of her jet earring and it bounced off the dressing table and rolled onto the carpet.

"Rats!"

On her hands and knees, she patted the thick pile looking for the little silver barrel. As her fingers closed around it she felt a pop at her knee and a run slithered up her thigh.

"Damnation!" She sat back on her heels and looked upward. What next?

Relax, she told herself. But she couldn't relax. The idea of going to bed with a man for the first time in years had her totally unstrung. She took a deep breath, quickly secured the earring, and put on an identical pair of hose. Just as she stepped into her shoes, the doorbell rang.

Picking up a lightweight black wrap and her evening bag, she went to answer it. Why, she wondered as she went, had she allowed herself to get in this state? Was any man worth the hassle?

When she opened the door and saw Wick, her silent reply was an unequivocal yes. His sensual aura enveloped her and his slow smile made her go warm all over. Instead of his usual casual attire, he was dressed in a dark suit, white shirt, and yellow tie that was the shade of spring butter.

His gaze swept over her and his smile broadened. "Beautiful," he drawled.

Her breasts swelled as his eyes lingered over the low V of the blouse. She resisted the urge to tug the supple fabric together. Instead, she smiled. "Thank you. And you look very handsome yourself. Would you like to come in for a drink?"

"If I came in, we might miss dinner entirely."

She laughed.

As they walked to his Corvette, she was keenly aware of his hand at her back and the brush of their bodies with each step. He helped her into the low-slung sports car, and her skirt slid up to reveal too much of her long legs.

As she tried to tug it back down he chuckled and stayed her hand. "Leave it. You have fantastic legs." His palm made a slow pass down the dark nylon from thigh to ankle and back again.

She raised an eyebrow. "Dinner?"

He sighed. "Ah, yes. Dinner."

Obviously she wasn't the only one with seduction in mind tonight. The air seemed filled with magic; the lights seemed brighter, and the soft music filling the car, sweeter.

At the Rooftop, a supper club on the twenty-fifth floor of the Shane Hotel, they had a window table, intimate and candle lit. The wine was perfect, crisp and chilled. The veal was succulent, the asparagus tender, the potatoes light and creamy on her tongue.

During dinner they shared laughter and quiet conversation, and looked out over the city's skyline. Two or three times the thought crossed her mind that she should explain about her smoking before things went any further—and they seemed to be on the verge of further. But either the time didn't seem right or their eyes would meet and the thought would be lost in a sea of sensual awareness.

Passing up dessert, they wandered into the adjoining lounge where a trio played, and they danced to a slow medley of old favorites. Wick held her close, and she could feel his breath against her ear. They fitted together like the proverbial hand and glove. Being in his arms was absolutely heaven. She could have stayed like this for hours, but she knew time was running out. Soon they would leave and they would . . .

She had to tell him now.

"Wick?"

"Hmmm?"

"We need to talk."

He laughed softly and the sound vibrated through her body. "We've been talking."

She sighed. "I mean serious talk." She pulled away and looked up at him. "I think that two people who . . . well, I believe that relationships should be based on complete honesty, don't you?"

He tensed and his smile faded. "It's usually a good idea. Did I tell you I like that dress you're wearing?"

"About ten times. Wick, I—"

He glanced around the hazy room. "This smoke is getting to me."

Dread weighted her stomach like an anchor. She swallowed. "Me too."

"Let's get out of here. I have something I want to show you."

Taking her hand, he gathered her bag and her wrap and whisked her toward the elevator. But instead of going down, they went up.

"I thought we were on the top floor," she said.

"Nope. And I have a surprise for you. Like surprises?"

"Sometimes."

The elevator pinged and the doors slid open. They were on the roof. Still holding her hand, he led her to the high railing that surrounded the edge.

She stretched her arms along the rail and lifted her face to the stillness of the night sky. "It's beautiful up here. The closest thing Houston has to a mountain."

Leaning out, she looked at the glowing outline of the city and the ribbons of streets and freeways dotted with red and white lights of fast moving traffic.

"When I was a little girl, I wanted to live on top of a mountain."

"What made you change your mind?"

"I considered moving to Colorado when I finished my doctorate at the University of Virginia, but my grandmother was ill and David and I came here instead."

"And later?"

"After Gram died, the time didn't seem right. David was settled in school with new friends, and my practice was established. I really do like Houston, but sometimes I miss having rugged peaks to climb. There's a power to them that draws me. It's strange since I've never lived in the mountains, but I often visited them when I spent summers with my parents. Among my fondest memories are Greece and Peru. Have you ever been there?"

He shook his head.

"My favorite place in Greece was a high hill above the temple of Delphi. The view was magnificent. I can understand why the ancient Greeks called the area the navel of the world. And the Peruvian Andes take your breath away. I once stood on a wall in Machu Picchu and spread my arms like wings, ready to fly. My father yanked me back just as I was about to jump."

He laughed. "I knew you were the adventurous type. Ever been to the Alps?"

"No, but I've always planned to go someday. I love the Rockies too. Ron and I went skiing in Colorado on our—" She paused and looked away.

"On your honeymoon?"

She nodded. "I haven't been skiing in a long time. I used to be darned good at it."

"I'm a pretty darned good skier myself. We'll go this winter if you like."

"You're on, but, as I said, it's been a long time. For a lot of years my life has been incredibly mundane. I'll probably have to start on the bunny slopes and work my way up."

As she watched what looked like toy cars on the street below, Wick's hand moved slowly up her spine. "It will all come back to you," he said. "Some things we never forget. Just relax and it happens automatically."

His words were low and suggestive, his hand, broad and warm. She had the definite impression that the topic had strayed from skiing.

He took her shoulders and turned her toward him. Muted sounds of cars and people below faded away as he lifted her face.

"I've been wanting to kiss you all night."

The first touch of his lips to hers was a gentle testing. Then his mouth became bolder, and his arms pulled her close against him.

Now. She had to tell him now.

"I want you, Maya. I ache with wanting you," he murmured against her ear.

"I want you too."

"Are you sure?"

"I'm sure. But first, Wick, there's something I have—"

He silenced her confession with a kiss. "Later."

"But—"

He kissed her lips and nibbled his way down her throat. "Later."

She sincerely intended to tell him about her smoking problem before the night progressed. She really did. But the incredible things he was doing to her with his hands and his mouth made it impossible to string two coherent words together. Nothing else seemed important at the moment. Giving herself up to sweet sensation, good intentions were swept from her head.

At last he pulled away. "I don't think this is the right place for what I have in mind. Come on. It's time for your surprise." He took her hand and strode across the rough surface of the roof.

"Slow down." She laughed as she hurried behind him, tugging on his hand. "I have on high heels."

He slowed his step. "Sorry, I'm impatient." His arm slid around her waist, and he bent to kiss her cheek.

"I thought the extraordinary view was the surprise."

"No, there's more." He grinned. "An even better view."

When she saw where he was leading her, she gasped and froze in her tracks. "It's a . . . it's a . . ."

Looking pleased with himself, he nodded.

He tugged her forward, but her feet were rooted

to the spot where she stood. Not for all the oil in Saudi Arabia could she have moved.

"Honey," he said, "you're shivering. Are you cold?"

She strained to give him a sickly smile. He whipped off his jacket and draped it over her shoulders. Hugging her close, he asked, "Better?"

Looking up at him, she forced her lips away from her teeth again, then glanced back at the hulking horror squatting before her, hoping that it had been a figment of her imagination. It wasn't. It was still there.

A terrible sinking feeling washed over her as she stared at the giant blue-and-white mosquito, with long rotors instead of wings, perched on the roof.

It was a helicopter.

This one probably would be considered a very fine piece of machinery as helicopters went, but she hated the things. More than hated them. They scared her witless.

"Very nice," she finally managed to say. "Yours?"

A slow, proud grin spread over his face as he nodded. He tugged her forward another step.

She balked. "I can see it well enough from here."

He laughed and pulled her toward the door of the craft. "Have you ever been up in a chopper?"

"No, and I'm not likely to in the next hundred years or so. I don't like helicopters."

The truth was that since Ron had died in a crash, she'd been phobic about helicopters. It was the only real phobia she had—well, snakes made her squirm sometimes. But even hearing the distinctive *whop, whop* noise of helicopter blades in the distance made her skin crawl. Planes didn't bother her—indeed, she enjoyed flying—but the idea of going up in this tiny bit of fiberglass and metal was terrifying. And she was sure that was his intention.

"Come on. I promise that you'll love it. The view is fantastic."

She refused to budge. "No. Not for a million dollars."

"At least come sit in Betsy. I'll explain how she works."

"I don't care how Betsy works."

"At least look inside."

With her protesting every step of the way, he installed her in the passenger seat of the tiny compartment. Her misery mounting by the second, she waited until he climbed into the pilot's position. The seats were so close together that only two inches separated them. She gave the cramped interior a cursory glance and shuddered.

"Okay, I've looked." She started to get out.

"Whoa!" he said, laughing and reaching for her. "Not so fast."

He pulled her to him and gave her a warm, slow, thought-chasing kiss. As his lips moved over hers and his tongue teased its way inside her mouth, she sighed and savored the sensual delight that his kisses always sparked in her.

His mouth left hers and went to her throat, trailing a tantalizing path down the skin bared by the neck of her blouse. At the valley of the opening, the tip of his tongue made small, slow circles, and his hand slid beneath her skirt to caress the curve of her outer thigh inspiring a potent yearning inside her.

"I want you, Maya," he said softly. "I'm crazy with wanting you. I need to feel your skin, naked and warm against mine."

His words were an erotic stimulant, and she

threaded her fingers through his thick, coarse hair. "Yes," she whispered, "I want that too."

"Come fly with me," he murmured against the swell of her breasts.

When his words registered in her desire-fogged brain, she stilled, then closed her fingers around handfuls of blond hair and yanked his head back. She glared down at him. "I'm *not* going up in this damned thing."

Looking as innocent as a child, he smiled up at her. "It's safer than a Harley."

She cocked an eyebrow. "Somehow that's not reassuring." She pushed him away and grabbed the door latch. He held her back. "Wick, listen to me. I'm not kidding. I'm not going to ride in this helicopter."

He only laughed. "That's what you said about the Harley, and you loved it. You can't know if you don't like something if you haven't tried it. Come on, give it a shot. I have a special destination in mind."

He peeled her fingers from the handle, brought them to his lips, then laid them on her thigh with a gentle pat.

She had hoped to extricate herself from the situation without making a fool of herself, but at the thought of flying in a helicopter, her anxiety picked up speed. Through dry lips she whispered, "I can't. I can't do it." She reached for the door again.

Chuckling, he hauled her back. "Sure you can. For a lady who once tried to fly off a mountain, a helicopter ride is a piece of cake."

He gave her a brief kiss and buckled her in, but he must have seen the panic in her eyes, for after the strap was secure, he tilted her face to his.

"Maya, I won't let anything happen to you. I'm a very good pilot. Trust me, you'll be as safe as a baby in its cradle. Okay?"

She closed her eyes and was silent. He waited.

True, she'd never ridden in one, but most people spent entire lifetimes without flying in one of the blasted things. Her fear of helicopters had never really interfered in her life. Consequently, very few—only those in her immediate family—knew how serious her qualms were. It was, to say the least, embarrassing for a psychologist to suffer from the very affliction she sought to cure in others. Wick seemed to have found all her weak spots.

Struggling to maintain control of her stampeding emotions, she opened her eyes and looked at him. Eyebrows raised slightly, he waited for her answer.

She tired to ignore the little prickles of fright breaking out on her scalp and forced herself to use logic. Wick was a helicopter pilot, and if she intended to pursue this flaming affair with him—and she did—perhaps it was time she faced her unnatural fear of the craft. Though it was not a method she preferred, flooding by being immersed in the frightening situation was a viable behavior modification technique. And there was no time like the present.

Put up or shut up, Dr. Stephens.

She took several deep breaths and gave a curt nod. "Okay. Let's do it."

He patted her leg. "Good girl. A little nervous?"

"That is a gross understatement. But let's rip the bandage off."

His brows drew together. "The bandage?"

She stuck out her bottom lip and blew out a

puff of air that ruffled her bangs. "There are two philosophies about the proper way to remove a bandage taped to a skinned knee. Slowly easing it off a little at a time, and jerking it off in one quick rip. Either way it's going to hurt."

He laughed. "I've always been a ripper myself. But don't worry. This won't hurt a bit. You'll find the view breathtaking."

She didn't believe a word he said.

Wick buckled his own harness and started the engine. When the rotors whined to life, Maya gripped the seat so hard, her fingers hurt. The helicopter vibrated as much as the Harley and was just as noisy. She almost tore off her seat belt and fled, but her fingers wouldn't move from the grip she had on the seat.

"I have to let it warm up for a minute," he shouted over the roar.

He snapped a pair of earphones from a hook behind them and motioned for her to do the same. When she didn't move, he set a pair over her ears.

"It cuts down the noise, and we can talk." He spoke briefly with a faint, disembodied voice on the radio, then said, "Here we go."

They began to rise and her dinner threatened to rise with the lift of the craft. She squeezed her eyes shut, and every muscle in her body was stiff.

Wick chuckled. "You can't see anything with your eyes closed."

She opened her eyes and, when he made a swooping maneuver over the freeway, she quickly shut them again and swallowed a squeal clawing up her throat.

Please, Lord, she prayed, *get me down in one piece, and I'll never cheat on my diet again. I won't swear when my car dies, and I'll give an extra thousand dollars to the women's shelter. I'll even give up smoking.* She tried to think of other things she could bargain with, but a tourniquet of fear tightened around her mind and no thoughts trickled through.

They must have flown over the city since Wick called out the names of various buildings and talked about fairylands of twinkling lights, but she didn't look. Her heart pounded, her throat constricted, and a cold film of moisture broke out across her upper lip. She tried to fight the trembling that started with her stiff knees and was fast spreading to the rest of her body, but, despite her best efforts, she shivered like a wet Chihuahua.

"Now, it isn't as bad as you imagined, is it?" he asked.

It was a thousand times worse! If some rational part of her brain hadn't diagnosed a panic attack, she would have been sure that she as having cardiac arrest.

"We're coming up on the University of Houston. Look, isn't that fantastic?"

She tried to control her breathing so that she wouldn't hyperventilate; she tried to think of God and country. But as Wick droned on about the sights below, all she could focus on was that they were suspended in the sky by only two putt-putting little blades. And if those blades stopped, they would drop like a rock into the cascading pool in front of the university's administration building.

Clenching her teeth, she endured a few minutes longer. It seemed like an eternity. She tried to contain her anxiety, open her eyes and act like a normal human being instead of a spineless hysteric. But when she peered through the Plexiglas bubble up into the night sky and down to the highway they were following, bile rose in her throat, and the top of her head felt as if it were about to blow off. Her panic escaped in a whimper, and she grabbed his thigh with a grip like an eagle's talons.

"Maya, what's wrong?" He sounded alarmed.

"I'm about to have a screaming fit and be sick all over your helicopter. Get me down!"

"Hold on, honey. We're almost there."

"Get me down, *now*!"

"Just another couple of minutes. Take deep breaths."

"I know how to breathe, dammit! Get me out of this thing!"

Six

Wick went cold all over when he realized how scared Maya was. She was such a gutsy, together lady, he never dreamed of a reaction like this. He figured that the helicopter would be like riding the Harley, if she tried it, she'd like it. What a first-class fool he was! He could have kicked himself from here to Singapore for his idiocy.

"Hang on, babe. I'll have you down in a minute," he said, trying to soothe her with his voice and wishing to hell he could take his hands off the controls and hold her.

He searched the area for a site to set Betsy down, but the pad at his place on the bay was the closest, and only another few miles away. When he spotted the landing area, he breathed a relieved sigh.

"We're almost there, honey."

He'd wanted tonight to be perfect—a romantic dinner and a flight over the city, then wine and candlelight on the deck to set the mood for the first time they made love. Hell, face it, he'd wanted to show off and impress her. But he'd screwed it up royally. Would she ever forgive him? He clenched his teeth and called himself every profane name in his vocabulary—and, even before throwing in a few Spanish and Chinese ones, it was an extensive list.

He set the chopper down as gently as a cherry on whipped cream, and, as soon as he was able to let go of the controls, he unbuckled his harness and reached for her. "We're on the ground, sweetheart. We're on the ground."

She flung herself into his arms. "Thank Heaven!" She gasped air into her lungs and melted against him.

He could feel her heart pounding, and she was shaking like an Alaska quake. "I'm so sorry, honey. I'm so sorry." For several minutes he held her, stroking her back and murmuring soothing words. "Let's get you out of here."

She whimpered when he pulled away, and he cursed silently. As quickly as he could, he shut down the chopper and ran around to open the door for her.

As he helped her out, she almost collapsed against him. After a nervous attempt at a laugh, she said, "I think my legs have turned to spaghetti. I feel like such a fool."

"I'm the damned fool."

He swept her up and, with her arms clinging to his neck and her head buried under his chin, he strode toward the door of the small weathered-cedar house on the water. At the door, he cursed again as he rattled the knob.

"The door's locked and the key's in my pocket. Do you think you can stand up for a minute while I unlock it?"

She took a deep breath and nodded. He let her down and, keeping one arm securely around her, opened the door.

She wasn't fine. He could feel her trembling still as she pressed against him, her arms circling his waist, holding him tightly as if she couldn't get close enough.

"Where are we?"

"At my weekend house in Kemah."

He swung her into his arms again and went inside. Still holding her, he sank down on a large, low couch and cradled her close. The sliding glass doors were exposed, the drapes drawn open, and an outside light joined with the full moon to reflect over the gentle ripples of the bay and spill into the room as the two sat huddled together in the soft shadows.

He slipped off her shoes and tossed them aside. His warm, sure hand stroked the silky length of her leg; his lips brushed across her auburn hair, murmuring reassurances.

Maya kept her face pressed against his broad chest, her arms locked around his strong, solid body. Never could she remember feeling so vulnerable, so desperate, and his presence, his maleness was the secure anchor in the turbulent, dark swell of her emotions. The distinctive scent of him surrounded her, and she felt the powerful beat of his heart pounding in unison with hers.

The frantic desperation of her terrifying experience clung to her still; the adrenaline rush continued to course through her blood. She wanted to draw from his essence, blend into his strength. Her arms tightened around him, but not tight enough.

"Wick, Wick," she whispered, and lifted her face to his.

Faint light silvered his tiger eyes and cast shadows across his face, etched with despair and another, rawer expression. Her breath caught; her heart stumbled. The two-sided coin that held fear and passion only a pulse beat apart spun and rolled. Conditions shifted like the slight turn of a kaleidoscope into a new, vibrant pattern.

The switch was so quick, so overwhelming that it seemed irrational, but in the primitive part of her brain that governs basic emotions, her terror had served as an aphrodisiac.

Desire sprang up to displace fear, but this transformed emotion was just as frantic, just as merciless and consuming in its onslaught.

Suddenly she was eager to taste him, feel him, desperate to fill her mind and body with him. Her hand moved upward and tangled in his hair. She pulled his head down and, with a low cry, her open lips reached for his. Her tongue tasted and probed the rich, moist heat of him. Her mouth swallowed his deep groan and reveled in the sparks flashing over her as his hands slipped over her body, boldly, wildly, as with a raging need to touch and explore and brand every part of her.

Wanting to feel his bare skin with her fingers, she whimpered and slid her hands under his jacket to his shoulders, trying to peel his clothes away. He shed the coat and his tie, throwing them aside and returning to her mouth with hungry urgency. She worked at the buttons of his shirt while he opened the single buckle fastening her top and parted the fabric.

"Maya, Maya mine . . ." His words were a muffled moan as he buried his face in the valley of her breasts and rubbed his cheeks against the flesh that swelled over the lacy bra she wore.

Her back arched, and she was lost in sensation as his tongue laved the top of her breast, and his hand dragged down the cup to free her nipple to his mouth. It was sweet madness.

Impatiently she tugged at his shirt. "I want to taste you. I want to feel your skin against mine."

He uttered a guttural sound and ripped his shirt open. Buttons pinged against the glass and landed on the carpet. Before he could return to her breasts, she was on him like a tigress, sinking her mouth in the hollow of his throat, licking the length of his collarbone, stroking the muscled expanse of his bare chest.

"More," she demanded as she pushed back his shirt and bit his shoulder. "I want more."

"Lord, woman," he groaned, "you set me on fire."

In one swift motion he was on his feet with her in his arms, striding for the bedroom. He laid her in a pool of moonlight on the bed, but she didn't stay. Before his shirt was off, she was on her feet, unbuckling his belt.

Their clothes were shed in a frenzy of hot kisses and touching and urging.

Wick tried to hold back, slow their lovemaking, but she refused to allow it. She pulled him down to the bed with her and writhed against him.

"Now," she said. "I want you inside of me, now."

"Easy, love." He stoked wispy tendrils from her damp forehead as he lay angled across her, raised on one forearm. "I have to protect you first."

He moved away for a moment, then was back to trail his tongue between her breasts and to her navel, pausing for nibbling forays along the way, tickling with his mustache until she was mindless with wanting.

"Wick, *please*."

"It's been a long time for you, hasn't it?" His tongue drew slow circles around her breast.

"A very long time."

His hand slid along the curve of her calf, then nudged her knees apart and continued a slow path up the inside of her thigh. "I don't want to hurt you. I want to be sure you're ready."

Higher, his fingers caressed a tender, aching spot. Her belly contracted and she sucked in a gasp. "I'm ready. Believe me, I'm ready."

He laughed. "I think you're right, love."

He moved to kneel between her legs, lifting her hips with one hand and stroking her breasts and torso with the other.

"Wick," she pleaded as he teased her.

His topaz eyes met hers and he smiled. "Come, love. Come fly with me."

He lifted her hips higher and began to enter her slowly, gently. But she would have none of his gentleness. She wanted his fire. Grasping his buttocks, she quickly thrust upward until she was filled with life, and the sensation was so wondrous, it stole her reason. She cried out and pulled him closer, deeper.

Thoughts of gentleness fled, and their joining became a lusty, primal striving of slick, hot bodies demanding and conceding, advancing and retreating. They strove on and on amid ragged breathing and cries of pleasure and gasps of praise to blissful release.

When the last spasms of passion were spent, Wick remained over her, quiet, bracing his weight on his fists, his chin to his chest. Maya felt drops of his sweat fall on her breasts and slowly blend with her own to trickle onto the bed.

She reached up to wipe the moisture from his brow with her fingers. He raised his head to look at her, and the awed expression on his face made her smile.

"I have never"—he kissed her lips—"never"—he kissed her again—"had an experience like that in my life. Are you a sorceress as well as a hypnotist?"

She laughed. It felt good to laugh. And it felt good to make love with a man again. "Not that I know of."

He kissed her again, a slow, sweet kiss. "Lady, you're something else." He rolled to his back and pulled her close so that she lay with her head on his shoulder, her leg over his, and her hand splayed on his chest. "I don't have words to describe how you affect me." He absently stroked his hand up and down her forearm. "You're sensational. Phenomenal."

She grinned. "You're no slouch yourself."

"I never dreamed that a psychologist would be so . . . uninhibited, so . . . wild."

"Disappointed?"

"Hell, no. Just surprised. Pleasantly surprised." He hugged her.

"They say older women make better lovers."

"You got that right."

Maya felt a twinge of regret at his response, then berated herself for being coy. The cold facts were that she was forty years old, and Wick was probably used to much younger partners, women with taut, unmarked bellies. Suddenly she felt exposed and embarrassed. She reached for the edge of the spread to cover her nakedness.

Wick sat up. "Are you getting chilly? I'm not doing a very good job of taking care of you tonight, am I?" He shifted to pull the covers back for her and climbed between them as well. When they were under the sheets, he pulled her close to him again. "Can you ever forgive me for forcing you to fly in the helicopter? I—"

She laid her fingers over his lips to silence. "You had no way of knowing that I have a phobia about helicopters."

"Is that what it was? A phobia?"

She nodded. "Complete with a first-class doozy of a panic attack. Who knows? The flooding may have worked. I won't know until I try it again."

"Flooding? What flooding?"

"It's a type of psychological treatment. The person with a phobia is deliberately thrust into the most threatening situation possible, flooded with anxiety-producing stimuli. Do you remember when Indiana Jones was thrown into the pit of snakes? That's flooding."

"It seems a little extreme to me."

She laughed. "Many people would agree, including me. It's not something I ordinarily recommend. But sometimes it works."

He raised up and looked at her. "You mean you may be over your fear of helicopters?"

"Perhaps."

He lay back down and continued stroking her skin. For a while they were quiet, content to be close. "What causes phobias?"

"In many cases we never know. They remain illogical, obsessive fears, and we treat the symptom instead of the cause. In my case I know. My husband, Ron, was a helicopter pilot in Vietnam. He flew rescue missions. Two weeks before the end of his second tour of duty, he was shot down. He died in a helicopter."

For a moment he didn't comment. Their breathing and the muffled calls of night creatures around the bay were the only sounds in the stillness.

"That was a long time ago," he said.

"Yes, a very long time ago."

A few minutes later he stopped stroking her arm, and his respiration became slow and regular. She lay awake for over an hour, wondering if she was letting herself in for heartache with Wick McCall. He and Ron were so much alike, it was scary.

No, nothing serious would come of their relationship. He was too young for her to consider any kind of permanent liaison with him. Later, Wick would meet a nice young woman and have a family. This was, she reminded herself, only a middle age fling, a chance to experience a last "flaming affair" before settling back into her complacent lifestyle.

Something tickled her nose and she batted it away. It happened again, and she gave another swat and turned over, pulling the sheet over her head. A hand tugged it away.

"Wake up, sleepyhead. It's almost noon. Are you going to sleep the day away?"

Maya opened one eye and squinted at the smiling man who leaned over her. "I certainly didn't get any sleep last night."

He gave her a wicked grin. "Are you bragging or complaining?"

She laughed and sat up in bed, pulling the covers up across her breasts. Her pulse quickened at the sight of Wick, tousle-haired and sun-bronzed, who wore only a pair of faded madras shorts. "I'm not complaining, but we old ladies need more rest than you young bucks."

"Don't give me that. You about wore me out. Brunch is almost ready. And we have time for a little sailing this afternoon. Do you like boats?"

"I like them fine, but if you recall, the only thing I have to wear is a very rumpled crepe dress."

"No problem." With a motion of his head, he indicated a large chest across the room. "The bottom drawer is filled with all sorts of extra things my sisters and nieces keep here. Or you can rummage around in my stuff for something."

"Do I have time for a quick shower?"

He shot her a lascivious leer. "Sure. Want some company?"

She cocked an eyebrow and stifled a grin. "No, thanks. I'm hungry."

He gave an exaggerated snap of his fingers. "Shoot." He stood there waiting and grinning. "Well," he said finally, "aren't you going to get up?"

"When you leave."

His brows shot up. "What? My uninhibited psychologist is modest?" He grinned. "After last night . . . and this morning, I don't think you have any secrets from me."

True, she told herself, but there was no way she was going to parade around in front of him without a stitch to cover her less than nubile figure. It was one thing to be naked together in a dimly lit room and quite another to be exposed in the harsh reality of daylight. Her eyes traveled the length of his taut, tanned perfection and she was doubly sure that she wasn't up to baring all. At least not yet.

"Humor me."

He bent and kissed her. "Just this once. How do you like your scrambled eggs?"

"Poached."

He laughed. "I got your purse from the chopper. It's on the dresser."

Wick whistled as he broke eggs into a bowl and beat them with a whisk. After the fiasco with the flight down, he'd been afraid that he'd blown his chances with Maya. But things had certainly turned around. His instincts had been right. Together they'd generated enough fireworks for a hundred Chinese New Years. Everything about her was perfect. Yep, she was the woman for him all right. He was sure of it.

While he waited for her, he automatically reached for the pack of cigarettes on the counter, then stopped as he realized what he was doing. Maya would have his head if she caught him smoking. He'd sneaked out on the deck while she was still asleep this morning and had a quick one.

The habit was harder to break than he figured. Damned hard, in fact. He was going to have to do something about it soon. Tony, one of his pilots, had told him about a new program he'd heard about, the Holden Method or the Holder Method—something like that. He'd look into it next week as soon as he got back from California.

He grabbed the pack and the lighter and stuck it in the back of a drawer behind an old sock and a bunch of flashlight batteries.

Frustrated with trying to hurry and being stymied in her search, a fine sheen of nervous perspiration broke out on Maya's face as she rummaged through the bottom drawer. There were several pairs of shorts and tops, but it seemed that not one of them was larger than a six. She located a white cotton sweat suit and tried it on. When she looked in the mirror, she nearly cried. Damn! She looked like a bratwurst.

Peeling it off, she tossed it back into the drawer. In desperation she pawed through Wick's things and dug out an old pair of gray sweatpants and a faded black T-shirt advertising Mexican beer. When she dressed, she looked in the mirror again and made a disgusted face at her reflection.

Why was it that in movie situations like this, the heroine always ended up all cute and perky in a "found" wardrobe that looked as if it had been designed for her by Calvin Klein? In the droopy pants and T-shirt she looked like a bag lady.

Oh, well. She shrugged. So much for wanting to look glamorous.

She longed for the comfort of a cigarette. She eyed the black evening bag on the dresser where she knew two lay wrapped in a tissue and tucked into the side pocket. Dare she? No, she hadn't told Wick yet. She couldn't.

Her chest felt tight and her stomach cramped.

Just one puff. Maybe two. She could open the window, lean way out, and blow the smoke outside.

No. She stiffened her spine and her resolve.

Using Wick's brush, she fixed her hair. When she picked up her bag to get her lipstick, the zippered side pocket enticed her with its hidden contents. She hesitated.

Oh, hell! She yanked open the zipper and grabbed the blue tissue and a pack of matches.

A few minutes later, feeling guilty as sin but infinitely more relaxed, she strolled into the kitchen. She'd gargled with mouthwash and doused her body with Passion from her purse spray.

Perhaps it didn't bode well for his taste, but Wick pecked her on the nose and told her how cute she looked in his clothes, bare feet and all. Her spirits rose several notches.

After they ate, he took her out on his boat for a brief sail around the bay. The day was perfect for sailing and Wick handled the craft skillfully.

She lay back, soaked up sunshine, and watched clouds as the boat silently skimmed the water's surface. Calling gulls and droning engines zipping across the distant expanse provided a pleasant, lulling background. She breathed deeply, savoring the distinctive pungency of fresh air and marine life around them.

"Coming here has been good for me," she said. "I can't remember when I've felt so relaxed and peaceful."

He smiled. "Then I'm glad we came. I know you work too hard. I imagine that being a psychologist is a high stress profession."

"It is. I think it's been getting to me more lately. I'm seriously considering taking a partner into my practice so that I can have more free time before I suffer total burnout."

"Good. I plan for you to spend a lot of that free time with me. We can come back here next weekend, if you'd like."

"I would. It's wonderful here. If this place were mine, I'd want to spend all of my time here just lolling around."

"Sometimes it's tempting. I spend most weekends in Kemah, but, for convenience, I have an apartment near Hooks Airport where my business is located."

The mention of his business cast a momentary pall over her mood. Helicopters. Tension tightened her stomach.

"I wish we could stay here longer," he said, "but I have to fly to California in a few hours." Her face must have shown her disappointment. "I'm scheduled to ferry a helicopter from Torrance to Houston for a customer. I'll be gone only a few days. Want to come along?"

She laughed. "No, thanks. I haven't progressed that far." Indeed, she wondered if she'd progressed at all. The idea of his flying one of those things for such a long distance disturbed her.

"You want to try flying Betsy back to Houston this afternoon, or do you want me to go get the car and pick you up?"

She thought for a minute. "You're a very good pilot, aren't you, Wick?"

He gave her a cocky grin and winked. "Sweetheart, I'm the best."

Could she do it? Could she gird up and force herself back into one of those god-awful eggbeaters with seats? She hated to make a fool of herself twice, but she'd never know if the flooding had worked if she didn't try. And it seemed important to overcome her fear if she and Wick were to continue their relationship.

"I think I'd like to try flying again. But if I feel that I can't make it, I'll tell you." She frowned. "Do we have to land on the hotel roof?"

He shook his head. "I had one of my men pick up the 'Vette and leave it at the airport."

With a sense of regret at leaving and a growing trepidation about the return trip, she helped Wick tie up the boat in the slip and went inside to dress.

Maya sat buckled into the passenger seat of the helicopter as the engine whined to life. Her anxiety had not magically disappeared, but it was not quite as bad as before.

"Okay?" Wick shouted over the noise.

She took a deep breath and commanded her body to relax. "Okay."

They put on headphones, and she closed her eyes. Gripping the seat, she began silently reciting a list of affirmations and positive self-talk.

I am calm and relaxed. Wick is an excellent pilot. Flying in a helicopter is a safe and pleasant experience.

The craft began to rise and her anxiety rose with it.

I am calm and relaxed. Wick is an excellent pilot. Flying in a helicopter is a safe and pleasant experience.

Sweat broke out on her upper lip, and her stomach contracted into a tight knot.

I am calm and relaxed. Wick is an excellent pilot. Flying in a helicopter is a safe and pleasant experience. I am calm and relaxed. Wick is an excellent pilot flying in a helicopter is a safe and pleasant experience. I am calm—

"Babe, are you okay?"

Eyes still squeezed shut, she shook her head vigorously.

"Relax, honey. I'm taking her down. Just relax."

A moment later they were on the ground, and Wick had her in his arms.

"I feel like such an idiot. A stupid, weak, incompetent, bloody, blooming idiot!"

"Shhhh, honey," he crooned, rubbing her back. "Don't worry about it. We've all got a hang-up of some kind or another."

"Yes, but—"

He kissed her quiet. "Are you afraid now?"

"No, but—"

He kissed her again. "Look around you." When she did, he asked, "Where are you?"

"In your helicopter, of course."

"Are you afraid?"

"No."

He grinned. "Then look how much better you are. Last night just looking at Betsy scared you to death."

She gave a shaky laugh. "Who's the psychologist here?"

Acting playfully smug, he said, "Just call me Dr. McCall."

Her laugh was genuine, hearty. "You're crazy."

"Yes, ma'am. About you." He gently kissed each eyelid, then her mouth.

With him brushing aside her apologies for inconveniencing him, Wick situated her back in the cottage. "Have a drink and watch some TV or sit on the deck and soak up some rays. I'll be back before you know it." He kissed her and left.

Grateful for his sensitivity, she poured herself a glass of wine and took a couple of sips. He was right; her phobia had diminished, but it hadn't disappeared. So much for flooding. Just thinking about having to fly any distance made her nervous, and thinking about Wick up in that contraption made her nervous too.

A cigarette. She needed a cigarette.

She smoked the one left in her purse, then hiked three blocks to a store and bought another pack. So much for Chelsea's kissing theory.

Seven

The light changed to green, and Maya pressed the accelerator of her recalcitrant station wagon. It gave two half-hearted lurches and died in the middle of a busy intersection. Impatient Monday morning drivers honked behind her as she ground the key and pumped the gas. Nothing.

"Oh, great! Just great!"

The only lucky thing was that there was a car dealership on the corner. She set the hazard lights blinking, grabbed her purse and briefcase, and dodged traffic to the curb. Charging straight for the Ford dealer, she cornered the first salesman she saw, a short, plump fellow with a bow tie and a wide smile.

"How much will you give me for that piece of junk sitting in the middle of the street?" she asked him.

He hitched his pants over a paunch that bulged out like a basketball hidden under his shirt, and, eyes narrowed and lips puckered, walked over to the window. "A free tow to the wrecking yard."

"Sold. What do you have that I can buy and drive out now?"

He waved his hand toward several models on the showroom floor. "You have anything particular in mind?"

She walked around looking at the shiny cars on display, bypassing sedans and grimacing at a station wagon and a van. A snappy number at the end caught her attention. White with a tan interior and wire wheels, the little convertible seemed to glow with a magical radiance. It beckoned her.

She circled it twice, climbed in the driver's seat, smelled the leather, and put her hands on the steering wheel. A convertible, especially one so small and sporty, was a totally illogical choice. She stroked the soft leather seat, ran her fingers along the dash. A four-door sedan was much more practical. She opened the glove compartment, looked in, then closed it. The Mustang was not at all in keeping with her image.

"I'll take it," she said. "Where do I sign?"

Just under an hour later Maya zipped into the parking garage of her office building. It would have taken less time, but she did a bit of dickering with the salesman. She might have been impulsive, but, after all, she wasn't completely crazy. Her hair was windblown and she was smiling. She'd missed her aerobics class, but she felt great.

When she entered the office, Camilla gave her a knowing look. "You've sure got a spring in your step this morning. You must've had a swinging weekend with the hunk."

Maya picked up the mail and glanced through it. "Ummm."

"Ummm, yes or ummm, no?"

"Just ummm. Don't you have some filing to do?"

"Nope. I'm all caught up. Did you do anything exciting with Wick?"

"We went to the Shane Rooftop Friday night for dinner and dancing."

"And what did you do Saturday night?"

"Washed my hair and read a murder mystery."

"Humph! Sounds like my man dropped the ball."

Maya smiled. "Wick had to go to California Saturday. But he called last night. He should be back sometime Tuesday evening, and we're going out Wednesday night. To McDonald's."

The secretary looked affronted. "*McDonald's?* Hasn't that dude got any imagination? There's nothing romantic about a Big Mac and fries."

"Oh, I don't know. To three- and four-year-old little girls, a hamburger with their handsome Uncle Wick is probably a real turn on." Maya laughed. "Wick already had plans and asked if I minded tagging along. He said the munchkins have to be home early, and we're going to catch a show at Rockefeller's later. Happy now, nosy?"

Camilla gave a nonchalant waggle of her head and picked a dead leaf from the philodendron on her desk. "If you're happy, Dr. S., I'm happy."

A brochure in the stack of mail had a red paper clip attached to it with a note saying: "READ THIS!!!" Maya glanced at the copy advertising the Holden Method and frowned. "Is this another one of your subtle messages?"

"Sounded interesting. They've been running ads in the newspaper all week. Guaranteed to have you off cigarettes in five days or your money back. They have an orientation session on Wednesday afternoon. Want me to see if I can get you an appointment?"

"But I have patients scheduled."

"I think I can do a little juggling. Want me to try?"

Maya tapped the brochure against her palm and thought for a moment. Since she fully intended to keep seeing Wick, she was going to have to do *something*. And soon. It was bad enough that she'd acted like a goose with the helicopter. The idea of confessing about smoking at this late date was completely mortifying. She handed the flier to Camilla.

"Do it."

Wind played havoc with Maya's hairdo, but she loved riding with the top down. And scarves were for sissies. Besides, she liked the feel of wind in her hair. It made her feel alive, gloriously uninhibited, and ten years younger. She flipped the collar of her white silk shirt up to a jaunty angle and tilted her chin.

When she stopped at a red light, a man in a black Porsche stopped in the lane beside her. He glanced over at her and winked. She gave a toss of her head and laughed out loud. Maybe the middle-age crazies had infected her personality, but her attitude had changed. The transformation felt sensational, and she planned to enjoy every minute of it.

Chelsea had been bug-eyed when she'd seen the convertible. "The old clunker finally went to car heaven, did it?" She had trailed her fingers along the white fender and said, "I see the fine hand of Wick McCall in this baby."

"I'll have you know that Wick had nothing to do with it. He's somewhere between here and California."

"Have things heated up between you two?"

Maya had tried to mask a smile. "Why are you and Camilla so interested in my love life? Voyeurs?"

Undaunted, Chelsea had laughed. "You don't have to say another word. I can see by the sparkle in your eyes that the blond-haired Zorro has made his mark. Grab the ring, sister-in-law. That man was made for you."

Made for her? Maya wondered. He was great lover material, but— She dismissed the whole thing from her mind.

Five minutes later she reached the building that was her destination. She parked, gave her hair a few swipes with a brush, and put the Mustang's top up. She considered having one last cigarette but decided against it. The Holden Method was going to work. Positive thinking was half the battle, and today was the first day of her new smoke-free existence.

With a confident tilt to her head and a swish of her skirt around her knees, she strode into the new atrium building on the North Loop. Its lush foliage smelled faintly of the rich, earthy scent of a greenhouse, and the water cascading from intricately sculpted metal fountains gave the open area a spalike feeling.

So caught up was she in watching water trickle from a delicately wrought copper leaf that she almost collided with a man at the elevator door. She turned, a "sorry" forming on her lips, then froze. Blood drained from her face.

"Wick!"

He looked as startled as she. "Maya!"

"Wh-what are you doing here?"

"I—I was going to ask you the same question."

"I'm here to see my CPA," she improvised quickly.

"I'm here to see a customer who's interested in buying a new JetRanger."

"Small world," they said at the same time.

The elevator doors slid open. Maya got on. Wick followed.

"Floor?" he asked.

"Uh . . . four." She could walk down one flight.

He punched two and four. The doors closed. They both faced front and stared at the indicator light.

She fiddled with her purse. "Good trip?"

"What?"

"Your trip to California, was it pleasant?"

"Oh. It was okay." He jingled the coins in his pocket.

The elevator was slower than Chinese water torture.

At last the doors opened. Wick hesitated a moment, then got off. "See you later, babe."

She gave him a little flutter of her fingers. "Five-thirty."

The doors slowly slid shut, and she expelled a long puff of air. That was a close call. Of all times for her to run into Wick. She'd never had such an awkward moment in her life. She'd treated him almost like a stranger. He must have thought she was demented.

Quickly she punched three and got off on the right floor. She went through a set of double glass doors to a large reception room resplendent with overstuffed chairs and the same tropical foliage that graced the downstairs. Several people were waiting.

"I'm Maya Stephens," she told the receptionist. "I'm here for this afternoon's orientation session."

The young woman with a French braid and designer glasses turned on a saccharine smile. "We're so delighted that you decided to try the Holden Method. The session will start in a few minutes. While you're waiting, would you fill out this questionnaire for us?" She handed Maya a clipboard with a form attached. "Return it to me, and we'll be commencing shortly."

Maya took the clipboard and sat in one of the plump chairs behind a large fiddle-leaf fig plant. She'd filled out the first four questions when she heard a familiar voice at the receptionist's desk. Her heart tripped. Drawing aside a branch of the plant, she peered through the broad leaves.

OhmiLord! She jerked her hand back and slunk down in her seat. Wick. What was he doing here? Had he followed her? The jig was up. She scrunched down farther in the chair, leaned closer to the fig tree, and held the clipboard up to her face so that only her eyes showed above it. Maybe he wouldn't see her.

Please, she prayed, *don't let him spot me.*

The powers that be must have been on a coffee break. Wick, clipboard in hand, walked to the chair directly across from her and sat down. Her eyes widened, and she tried to make herself invisible.

Wick dropped his pencil and reached to the floor for it. She felt his eyes travel up her legs, up her body, past the clipboard to the wide green eyes staring at him.

"Maya?"

She lowered her shield and forced the corners

of her mouth upward. He looked at her as if she'd sprouted antennae and an extra eye.

"What are you doing here?"

"I . . . What are *you* doing here?"

Like the motions of synchronized dancers, they each looked at the other's clipboard, then back at their own.

He shook his head mutely.

She sighed. "I think we need to talk."

"I think you're right. Let's get out of here."

They tossed their questionnaires aside and left the reception room. Neither said a word until they were at the elevator.

Wick spoke. "I could use a drink. How about you?"

She nodded. "And a cigarette."

"You got that right."

They looked at one another and burst out laughing.

In a dimly lit neighborhood bar two blocks from the offices of the Holden Method, Maya and Wick sat in a corner booth. Except for two employees and a man in a plaid shirt watching a soap opera on the TV behind the bar, the place was deserted. As soon as the cocktail waitress left to get their drink order, Wick took a pack of cigarettes from his jacket pocket, shook one out, and offered it to her.

"Thanks," she said, taking it.

He shook one out for himself and lit hers, then his. After they both blew out plumes of smoke, he chuckled. "I can't believe we've been sneaking around hiding the fact that we smoke from one another. Why didn't you tell me?"

"I was too embarrassed. Can you imagine how humiliating it is to conduct no-smoking sessions and be hooked on the damned things myself?"

He grinned. "Have you tried a good hypnotist?"

She laughed. "Several. Unfortunately, I'm always critiquing their techniques, and I'm a lousy subject. Why did you keep your smoking secret from me?" She drew her brows together and studied him. "You came to the session at Fairmont Oil for yourself, didn't you?"

He nodded. "But I discovered I was more interested in the psychologist than in quitting cigarettes. *You* mesmerized me."

The waitress returned with their drinks. After they'd taken a sip, Wick asked, "Are you angry with me for getting to know you under false pretenses?"

"How could I be? I'm just as guilty as you. I kept meaning to tell you, but the opportunity didn't seem to present itself. I've been trying to quit for months and nothing seems to work."

"I know the feeling." He told her about his father's illness and his promise to his mother. "Got any ideas on how we can kick the habit?"

She grinned. "I was your best bet and you blew it. I'm really very good at helping other people, but I'm lousy at helping myself." She told him about all the methods she'd tried. "I think if I attacked it with a total modality program on a deserted island with no way to get to cigarettes for about a week, I could lick it."

"Hmmm." He took a swallow of his drink and drew wet spirals on the table with the bottom of his glass. "I can provide the island if you'll outline the program."

"I was just hypothesizing. There's no way I can leave my practice for a week right now."

"Why not?"

"I have several patients with critical problems. They depend on my being there to help them."

"Won't the same problems be there a week later?"

"Yes, but—"

"How long since you've had a vacation, Maya?"

"About three years."

"I think it's time you took one. How about next week?"

"There's no way."

"I'll bet Camilla can think of a way."

"No doubt."

"Is this the lady who told me only a few days ago that she was getting burned out? Maya, you owe it to yourself to take some time away. Let's go adventuring. My old diving buddy has a house on a small island in the Caribbean that is miles away from the nearest inhabitants. It has white sandy beaches and the water is so blue, it's unbelievable. It's fantastic for scuba diving." He leaned over close to her and nuzzled her ear. "We could have a week by ourselves with nothing to do but swim and lie in the sun"—he tugged at her lobe with his teeth—"and make love."

A sensual shiver slithered up her spine. It was tempting. Very tempting.

The tip of his tongue teased the inner rim of her ear. "What do you say?"

She wiggled as his tongue teased further. "You're not playing fair."

He gave a low, wicked chuckle.

"I'll see what I can work out," she said.

"Good girl."

*   *   *

Maya smiled as she watched Stephanie, the three-year-old, drag a french fry through a blob of catsup and put it in her mouth. A trail of red goo dribbled down her chin.

"Oooo," Holly said with all the superiority of her additional year, "gross."

Stephanie went still and her bottom lip puffed out.

Wick, who was sitting opposite Maya and flanked by the two blonde-haired moppets, wiped the messy chin. "Don't worry about it, pumpkin." He took another bite from his cheeseburger.

The younger child threw her arms around Wick's neck in a stranglehold. "I wuv my Unka Wick. He drives hewicoppers."

Not to be outdone, Holly hugged him too. "He took me for a ride on my birthday. We went wa-ay high."

"When I'm this many"—the little one held up four greasy fingers—"I get a birfday ride too. Right, Unka Wick?"

He grinned. "Right."

Stephanie looked at Maya and said seriously, "If you're a *very* good girl, maybe he'll take you for a birfday ride."

Maya laughed. "My birthday isn't for a long time."

"My birfday is in—" She looked at Wick.

"February," he supplied.

"Mine is July," Holly piped. "I ate mine all up. Can we go on the slide now?"

Stephanie bounced up and down. "The slide. The slide."

Wick looked at Maya and winked. "Are you finished with your salad and McNuggets?"

She grinned. "I ate them all up. Go ahead with

the girls to the play area. I'll clean the debris from the table."

"Oh, no. We have to clean up our own mess," Holly said. "Uncle Wick says we don't want people to think our mommy raises—"

"Pigs!" Stephanie said, and giggled behind her hands.

Wick checked to see that their hands were cleaned and made a swipe at a spot of catsup on the bib of Stephanie's pink overalls. When the table was cleared, the four of them went outside to the playground.

After the girls had frolicked for about fifteen minutes, Wick said, "Okay, rug rats, it's time to go."

Both children protested, but he held firm and herded them into the Jeep wagon. After the girls were buckled up in the backseat he turned to Maya and grinned.

"Now when have you had a more stimulating dinner date?"

She laughed. "I've enjoyed it. The girls are adorable."

On the way home the girls chattered about a variety of subjects, jumping from one eccentric topic to another. In the middle of their discourse Holly asked Maya, "Are you going to marry my Uncle Wick?"

Maya was stunned. Before she could reply with a suitable answer, Stephanie said, "No. *I'm* going to marry Unka Wick."

"You can't marry Uncle Wick, silly," Holly informed her sister. Maya hoped the subject was at an end, but Holly was not easily detoured. "My gramma told my mommy that it was about time my Uncle Wick found a 'spectable woman and got married. What's 'spectable?"

Wick burst out laughing. "*Respectable*, termite. Respectable means very nice." To Maya, he said, "The girls' grandmother is my oldest sister and had been concerned about my single state for years."

"Are you going to marry my Uncle Wick?" Holly persisted.

"No, sweetheart. Wick and I are just friends."

She was saved from further interrogation when the Jeep stopped in front of a small house in West University, a few blocks from her own.

"Come on in and meet my niece Kathy and her husband."

Wick took her hand, and they went up the walk behind the two little girls who were running to the door. Besides Kathy and Mark, there was an older couple in the living room. Wick introduced them as his sister Sara and her husband, Joe.

Although everyone was extremely polite as they chatted for a few minutes, Maya got the distinct impression that she was being evaluated. Sara, an older, feminine version of Wick with an abundance of gold bracelets and diamond rings, was especially cordial and looked pleased. Maya was uncomfortable with his sister's significant glances back and forth between them. She wanted to blurt out that she and Wick were only having a flaming affair and that she was *not* a candidate for his bride. Surely they could see that she was too old for the position.

When they said their good-byes, the girls insisted on hugging both of them.

"I think you're 'spectable," Holly said in a stage whisper as Maya bent down to her. "And your hair is very pretty." She stroked a long tress. "Just like Trixie's."

Wick burst into laughter.

"Trixie is an Irish setter," he explained when they were outside. "And I think your hair is much prettier." He gave her a kiss and installed her in the front seat.

"I don't think you should have introduced me to your family," she said as they drove away.

"Why not?"

"I think they're back there planning a kitchen shower."

He glanced over at her and grinned. "Would that be so bad?"

"Disastrous."

He started to comment, but seemed to think better of it and was silent for a few minutes as he drove.

About ten minutes before show time, they arrived at Rockefellers, a popular night spot on the edge of downtown. Housed in an old brick building that had been a bank many decades before, the room was crowded with noisy patrons crammed together at small tables, having drinks and waiting for the show to begin. A haze of smoke drifted around thick pillars, vestiges of the building's former incarnation, and upward to the high ceiling to hang like gray smog.

They were ushered to seats on the rail of the mezzanine with an excellent view of the stage. After they ordered drinks, Wick scooted his chair closer to hers and lit cigarettes for them both. As the houselights and spots signaled the opening number, he laid his hand on her thigh and kept it there.

Even though she loved k.d. lang, Maya found

that she was only half listening to the singer's performance. Most of her attention was on the man beside her. His palm slid down her thigh to her knee, circled it twice, then slid back up again. He repeated the absent stroking while k.d. sang throaty, passion-stirring blues songs. She squirmed and stilled his hand with hers. She reached for another cigarette.

The show was only half over when he leaned over and brushed her cheek with his lips. "I've missed you," he whispered. "Why don't we cut out of here?"

She nodded.

"Your place or mine?"

"Not mine, Chelsea's there."

"Let's make it mine."

Later Wick reluctantly agreed to take her home when she explained she had an early session with a patient the next morning. It was well after midnight when Maya tiptoed toward her bedroom, trying not to wake Chelsea. She needn't have bothered playing mouse, for her sister-in-law poked her head out her door as Maya rounded the corner.

"What are you doing home?" Chelsea asked.

"I live here, remember?"

Undaunted, Chelsea followed her into her bedroom and sat Indian fashion on the chaise while Maya undressed. The younger woman grinned. "I was hoping that you had decided to stay over with a friend."

"With a friend? Or with Wick?"

Chelsea shrugged. "Same thing. When is this flaming affair with you two going to ignite?" She hugged a needlepoint pillow to her chest and propped her chin on one edge. "I'll swear—" Her avowal stopped abruptly as her eyes fell to the front of Maya's blouse. She giggled.

"Aha! It seems that it's already ignited. Things getting serious?"

Maya looked down at the place where Chelsea had zeroed in and was mortified to see that the buttons were done up in the wrong holes. "Serious? Certainly not."

She turned her back and undid the blouse, tossing it into the hamper as she went into the bathroom. Quickly she finished undressing and donned her nightgown. While she slathered cleansing cream on her face, Chelsea, the pillow still hugged to her and one foot resting on the opposite knee in a stork pose, leaned against the door frame, watching her.

Annoyed with the reflection of Chelsea's amused expression, Maya snapped, "Why are you staring?"

"I'm just trying to figure out how, if nothing serious is going on with you and Wick, you got a love bite on your shoulder."

Automatically she clamped her hand on her right shoulder. *"Chelsea!"*

The blonde burst into laughter. "Gotcha! Now give."

Maya finished her nightly ritual before she said another word. With her sister-in-law on her heels, she walked to her bed, drew the covers back, and climbed in. "I have no intention of discussing the intimate details of my sex life with you or anyone, but I will say things have progressed considerably beyond hand-holding. As to our relationship being serious, there was never any possibility that it would be more than a mutually satisfying interlude."

Chelsea laughed and plopped down on the foot of the bed. "You can't put me off by playing supercilious psychologist. I'm not at all intimidated. I know you too well. Is he fantastic in the sack?"

Solemn, Maya raised her eyebrows and looked down her nose at the impish, expectant face. "Dy-na-mite."

Chelsea let out a whoop and tossed the pillow into the air. "I knew it! I knew you two would be perfect together. I've got dibs on being matron of honor this time."

"Matron of honor? Are you out of your gourd? I have no earthly intention of marrying Wick McCall."

"Well, why not? It may be a little early in the game, but I think it could very easily develop into something permanent."

"Chelsea, stop trying to play Cupid and listen to me. Wick and I are *not* perfect for one another. For one thing, he's too young for me." She held up her hand before Chelsea could protest. "I know. I know. You think three years is no big deal. But Wick is a very young thirty-seven, and I'm a very mature forty."

Chelsea rolled her eyes. "Get out your cane, Mother McCree."

Maya gave an exasperated sigh. "Anyway, age is not the major issue. Have you forgotten about the helicopters? I haven't."

"I thought you were getting over your phobia."

"Being able to sit in one, on the ground, for two minutes does not constitute a cure. The idea of going up in a helicopter still scares me spitless. And I'm not too fond of thinking about him zipping around in those eggbeaters either."

"Oh?" A knowing smile spread across the younger woman's face. "Care about him, do we?"

"Of course I care about him. I enjoy his company. He's a . . . special friend. But the possibility of there being anything permanent is totally out of the question. Totally. Completely. Unequivocally."

"Hmmm." Chelsea's eyes crinkled, and she drew her mouth up into a tight little bow. "Methinks the lady doth protest too much. Isn't that what you shrinks call a reaction formation?"

"Lord, deliver me from amateurs."

Wick lay in bed, staring at the ceiling and fighting the urge to smoke. The sheets beneath him and those tangled around his legs still smelled of Maya. His hand stroked the empty place where she had lain, and he wished for her warm, soft body instead of rumpled fabric under his fingers.

Are you going to marry my Uncle Wick? Holly's words clicked around in his mind like stones in a tumbler until the rough edges were smoothed off. Marry her? He tested and poked at the idea. With her answer to Holly and her comment about kitchen showers, Maya had squelched any such notion in a hurry. In fact, now that he thought about it, her quick "disastrous" had rankled a bit. More than a bit.

He punched his pillow and kicked at the sheets. Why would marriage to him be so bad? He kind of liked the idea himself. There was no doubt in his mind that he was fast falling in love with her. They'd be great together. They were certainly compatible in bed. And in other ways too. They liked a lot of the same things.

Except helicopters. And that was no big deal.

Mechanics didn't expect their wives to help fix cars, and surgeons never took their wives in the operating room. He flew helicopters, and she dug around in people's psyches. The thought of messing with somebody else's mind was probably scarier to him than helicopters were to her—which was okay, since that part of their lives was separate.

Marriage? Yes, for the first time in his adult life, he liked the idea. If Maya seemed a little lukewarm now, well, he'd just have to work on her some. It might take a couple of weeks, but she'd come around.

Eight

As she stood on the hotel balcony a gentle sea breeze ruffled the auburn strands of Maya's hair and tugged at the hem of her yellow sundress. She leaned against the stucco wall and gazed out at the white sugar sand beach of St. Thomas. Beyond, clear turquoise-tinted water shaded to striated lapis on the horizon, broken only by occasional white sails and humps of gray-green islands in the distance. She breathed deeply of the Caribbean morning, scented like freshly cut watermelon mixed with the salty air.

Finding a new partner for her practice and rearranging her schedule had taken almost a month, but, with Wick and Camilla's prodding, it had been done. Now she was glad that the two had pushed her. She hadn't realized how much tension she'd been carrying around until this morning. There was an ambience here in the islands that seemed to dissipate worries, melting them with the sun and scattering them with the breeze.

Wick came up behind her, wrapped his arms

around her waist, and kissed her shoulder. "Beautiful," he said, letting his lips linger.

"It *is* beautiful here. One of the most beautiful places I've ever seen."

He chuckled and the vibration of his mouth against her skin tickled. She shivered slightly. "I wasn't talking about the place, but the woman." He pulled her back closer to him and rested his cheek on her temple. "Though, you're right, it is beautiful here. The island where we're headed is even nicer because there'll be no one around but you and me." His hands slid up to capture a breast in each palm.

There was a knock at the door.

He made a low growl in her ear. "With no one to interrupt at awkward moments."

She laughed. "But that's our breakfast, and I'm starved."

He released her and admitted the waiter who delivered their morning meal to the small table on the balcony. When he left, Maya poured them each a cup of tea and added sweetener and lemon to her own.

Wick tasted his and frowned. "Are you sure I can't have a cup of coffee? I always like coffee in the morning."

She sighed. "And what do you like with your morning coffee?"

He grinned. "A cigarette."

"An important part of the program is breaking habit patterns. As you very well know, we need new routines and different surroundings to be successful."

"Why don't we have coffee and one last smoke before we jump into this total modality program?

Maybe it would be better to wait until we get to the island."

She gave him a stern look. "Uh-uh," she said, shaking her head slowly. "We agreed last night, when we had our last cigarette, that we would start this morning. In fact, I seem to remember that we had three or four 'last' cigarettes before we went to sleep. Besides, while you were in the shower, I shredded all the ones that were left in the pack and flushed them down the toilet."

He drank his tea.

When they had finished their rolls and fruit, Wick sat back in his chair and heaved a big sigh. "I still want a cigarette."

She gave him a wry smile. "I know the feeling. These should help." She extracted a vitamin bottle from her shoulder bag and shook out a B_6 for each of them.

As soon as he had swallowed the pill, he said, "It didn't help."

She laughed. "Give it some time. Wiggle the staple in your ear, and let's say the affirmation."

They both jiggled the "new and improved" little beads the acupuncturist had inserted inside their ears. Then they intoned together, "I am calm and relaxed. My desire for cigarettes has disappeared." They repeated the words ten times.

Wick stood up and crammed his hands in the pockets of his khaki shorts. "I feel like a damned fool chanting that stuff. Are you sure this is going to work?"

She looked up at him. "Getting a little testy already, are we?"

He laughed. "Sorry about that. Let's get our stuff together and get this show on the road."

"How do we get to our deserted island?"

"We can go to Crescent Cay either by seaplane, or"—he grinned—"we can rent a helicopter."

She shot him a withering look.

He cleared his throat. "Seaplane it is."

The plane circled the small island, a jade crescent lifted from the aquamarine sea. The convex side of the island was rough, with slate-gray rock rising up from the water's edge, but the concave curve formed a small cove with a white beach. The water surrounding the cay was so clear that the rock formations and pale sand on its floor appeared to be only inches below the glassy surface. On the side of a hill, a white stucco house with a red tile roof was tucked amid lush green vegetation and vibrant patches of pink, red, yellow, and orange.

They landed on the beach side, then taxied to a wooden pier and stopped. Wick tossed his duffel bag onto the dock with a thump, climbed out, and helped Maya from the plane.

He grabbed her bag and waved to the pilot. "Thanks, Harry. Pick us up here about this time Saturday morning."

The pilot waved his assent, then eased away from the shore. Maya and Wick both watched as the pontoons skimmed the surface, rose, and disappeared into the vast blue distance.

Wick turned to her. "Well, babe, it's just you and me for seven days. Think you can handle it?"

Her eyes scanned his laughing face with its tiger-eyed handsomeness that never failed to excite her, then turned to absorb the beauty of what could only be described as Eden. "I'll try to tough it out."

He laughed, slung his duffel over his shoulder and picked up her suitcase. "Let's go up to the house and get settled in."

At the end of the pier two very large German shepherds stood eyeing them. Maya stopped. "Are they friendly?"

"Only if they know you. Since my friend Bingo is gone so often, he decided to use guard dogs to keep intruders from making themselves at home or looting the place. Come on. I'll introduce you." He called the dogs over to them.

She looked askance at Wick as the dogs sniffed her hand. "Who names dogs Rin and Tin-tin?"

He laughed. "You'd have to know Bingo Hughes. He's quite a character."

"Who takes care of the dogs while Bingo is off on his jaunts?"

"He has a couple who lives here in a cottage near the house. But after they stocked supplies for us, they left this morning to visit their daughter on St. Croix."

They climbed stone steps up a winding path bordered by clumps of marigolds and cut through tropical vegetation. Sea grapes, palms, and grasses growing near the beach blended into breadfruit, cinnamon bay, yellow cedar, mango, tamarind, and mahogany trees. The leaves seemed crisper, sturdier here. They made a beguiling sound as the wind stirred through the limbs and mixed the low rustle with the higher pitched bird songs.

Along the way Maya stopped to look at several varieties of bromeliads and orchids. "My grandmother would have been envious. She was an avid gardener." Her fingers touched a firm petal here and there. "But she could only grow these in a greenhouse." She smiled up at Wick, who stood patiently waiting for her a few steps beyond. "This place is truly a paradise."

"I'm glad you like it. Wait until you see the view from the house."

The path curved around a magnificent flamboyant tree and ended on a veranda with stone balustrades and huge pots of red bougainvillea. A small, iridescent hummingbird flitted among the blossoms as they crossed the tile-paved area to the front entrance. Wick unlocked the intricately carved double doors and swung them wide. He dropped the bags by the entrance and took her on a quick tour of the downstairs.

An open foyer with stone and stucco arches led down two steps to a huge living-dining area. Completing the downstairs was a library and a large kitchen. Upstairs were two full suites and two smaller bedrooms with a bath between. Every room had big windows with fantastic views and were filled with a finely appointed mixture of contemporary and rustic Mediterranean furniture. The floors, antique tile and buffed to a soft patina, were covered with oriental rugs. Several vases of fresh cut flowers were scattered about the rooms.

After they unpacked their belongings in the suite where Wick told her he usually stayed, he asked, "Want to do a little snorkeling before lunch?"

"No, I'd rather have a cigarette. But I think snorkeling would be better." She grabbed her bathing suit and went into the bathroom.

When she was dressed in her new bikini, a black one gaily printed with stylized tropical fruit, she looked into the full-length mirror and groaned. She turned around, looked over her shoulder and groaned again, louder.

Wick knocked on the door. "Honey, are you all right?"

"I'm fine."

"Are you ready?"

"Not quite." She'd never be ready.

"I'll go on downstairs and get the equipment together. Okay?"

She made a disgusted face in the mirror. "Okay."

Now she understood why the department stores had such dim lighting in their dressing rooms. When she'd tried on the suit before she bought it, the bikini had looked fine. In fact, Chelsea had insisted it was "mucho, mucho."

It had to be the lighting. What else could explain how, in only three days, she'd gained twenty pounds—all in her thighs. She thrust her forearm against the wall and leaned against it. How could she walk around in front of Wick like this? Oh, the humiliation of it.

She tried lecturing herself about putting too much emphasis on physical attributes. She should be grateful that she had a healthy body. After all, wasn't what was inside more important than what was outside? If Wick McCall was so shallow that he couldn't overlook a few figure flaws, there certainly wasn't very much to his character. As her grandmother always said, beauty was only skin deep. Skin. Fat.

She groaned again and wished fervently that she could lock herself in the bathroom for the week. Why hadn't they decided to go to Alaska instead? She could have covered herself with fur pants and mukluks.

Changing into another suit wouldn't solve the problem. She sighed in disgust. For the past week of their relationship, she'd managed to keep from totally exposing her body to Wick in harsh light. And for someone who was as uninhibited as he was, it hadn't been easy. He'd teased her about being modest. Now the day of reckoning was here.

Well, she thought, the cold hard facts were that she was forty years old. There wasn't a blessed thing she could do about it.

She straightened her shoulders. Wick was just going to have to take her like she was. Who needed this kind of grief? She marched out of the bathroom like a knight off to slay a dragon. But she stopped along the way, grabbed her big purple stole with the fringe, and knotted it around her waist, sarong style.

Wick was waiting at the door with towels and a bag of equipment. With his little pink swimsuit and his tanned, rock-hard body, he looked like something out of a Chippendales' calendar. She tightened the knot of her shawl.

He smiled as his gaze flicked over her, then kissed her nose. "Very nice. I like your pineapples."

She looked down at the fruit print on her skimpy bra. "Thank you." He opened the door, and, as she sailed past, spine straight, chin up, she announced through gritted teeth, "I think you should know that I have a problem."

"A problem?"

She gave him a curt nod. "There's more of me than there is of this bikini bottom."

He wiggled his eyebrows. "Sounds interesting. Let me see." He grabbed a corner of the purple fringe, but she batted his hand away.

"Wick, this is serious. I look fat in this suit."

"You won't hear me complain." A lascivious grin spread over his face. "I'm partial to cantaloupes."

She turned to glare at him, but the whole thing

suddenly struck her as funny, and try as she might to suppress it, a snort of laughter exploded in her throat. "I'm laughing instead of crying."

"Oh, honey, you're not fat. Why are you so concerned? It doesn't seem like that big a deal to me." He threw an arm around her shoulders and pulled her close as they walked.

"*You* wouldn't. Your backside doesn't look like the main course at a luau."

He laughed and his hand slid down to her hip and patted it. "I like your backside just fine."

They spent an hour snorkeling in the warm clear water. Maya would have stayed watching the fascinating sea life longer but Wick was hungry, so they went back to the house for a quick shower and change of clothes. Sitting on the veranda, they lunched on crab salad and cold asparagus left by Bingo's housekeeper. Wick had three helpings plus a huge slab of coconut cake.

"Are you sure you don't want some cake?" he asked. "It's delicious."

Her mouth almost watered as she watched him shovel in a big bite. The scent of the fresh, sweet coconut was enough to make the strongest person's taste buds beg. "I'm sure it is, but I can't afford to start substituting food for cigarettes. I'll get as fat as a cow."

He mashed together the last few crumbs with his fork and ate them. Leaning back in his chair, he shook his head. "It's no substitute, believe me. I still want a cigarette."

Neither wiggling staples, reciting affirmations, chewing nicotine gum, nor a long walk around the island helped either of them much. Wick strode around the property at such a pace that she almost had to run to keep up with him. Rivulets of sweat ran down her face, which felt flushed and feverish, and her shirt stuck to her back. He said very little, and his few comments were terse and abrupt. Maya found herself snapping back at him.

When they were back at the house, he raked one hand through his hair and clenched and unclenched his fists. "Babe, I'm sorry that I'm being such a jerk, but I feel like I'm about to explode."

"Is your chest tight and does your stomach cramp?"

He nodded.

"Do all your muscles feel like you're stretched on a rack?"

He nodded.

"Do the tendons in your neck feel as if Godzilla and King Kong are playing tug-of-war with them?"

He nodded.

"Does the thought of never ever being able to smoke another cigarette in your whole entire life seem so overwhelming that you'd like to throw yourself off a twenty-story building?"

"Or shoot myself. Yes."

She sucked in a deep breath. "Me too."

"Oh, babe." He gathered her into his arms and they clung to each other.

By the night of the second day on the island, they were stalking around the house like caged animals. A magnificent tropical sunset came and went, but neither of them cared enough to watch it. Wick was miserable, and angry with himself. How could any man let something get ahold of him like this? He was acting like a bear. But he'd never been in such a state before. He felt doubly bad because he knew Maya was going

through the same kind of hell. He'd read somewhere once that, for some people, kicking cigarettes was worse than kicking heroin. He believed
it. He felt like he was about to come apart.

They'd put a movie in the VCR, but he didn't
have the foggiest notion what they'd been watching. Every nerve in his body was standing up and
screaming. He glanced over at Maya. She was sitting on the couch, stiff as a poker and with her
fingers laced together in a death grip. Here eyes
were closed, and she was taking deep breaths and
chewing fast on their special gum.

"That help?" he asked.

"Not a damned bit."

"I'm going to have a drink. A big one." He strode
to the bar and poured three fingers of bourbon.
Just as he raised the glass to his mouth she
grabbed his wrist.

"That's the worst thing to do. Let's say the affirmations again."

"To hell with those damned affirmations!"

He slammed the glass down on the tile counter
so hard that it shattered. Liquor splattered everywhere and dribbled onto the floor. The whole room
reeked of bourbon.

"Damn it! See what you made—" He froze when
he saw her face. She looked stunned, as if he'd
slapped her. All the anger drained from him. "Oh,
honey, I'm sorry." He pulled her into his arms and
started kissing her cheeks, her eyes, her nose.
"I'm so sorry. I'm acting like a short-tempered
fool. Please forgive me."

Her arms went around him, and she patted his
back. "I understand. Believe me, I understand."
She gave a bitter laugh. "Let's go to bed."

He pulled back and grinned down at her. "You

think we can find a way to take our minds off cigarettes for a while?"

She smiled, a slow, sexy smile. "We can try."

It was barely dawn when Maya awoke. She tried to go back to sleep—the longer she slept, the less time there was to wrestle with her debasing demon. Unfortunately, she was wide awake. She had thought that by now the urge for a cigarette would have abated somewhat, but it descended on her like a vulture picking at her insides. Not even the warmth of Wick's arm around her and his body pressed against her back distracted her obsession. It was the last thing she thought about before she went to sleep, and the first thing on her mind this morning. She'd even dreamed about smoking, and the dream had been so real that she could still smell the tobacco burning.

She turned over and looked straight into a pair of unblinking amber eyes. "What are you thinking?" she murmured.

He didn't hesitate. "That I'd sell my soul for a cup of coffee and a cigarette."

"So would I."

"It's stupid to put ourselves through this torture." He threw back the covers. "Bingo smokes. There are bound to be cigarettes stashed somewhere in this house, and I'm going to find them."

"I'll help you look."

He pulled on a pair of blue briefs and strode from the room. She scrambled into a robe and followed him. They searched Bingo's suite from stem to stern. They looked in every drawer, closet, cupboard, and cubbyhole in the entire house. Nothing. Not a cigarette or so much as a single shred of tobacco. They even tried the boat house.

Wick stood with one hand on his outslung hip looking totally disgusted. "Damn." He looked at the empty slot where she supposed a big boat was usually kept, then at the small outboard. "Marie and Paulo must have taken the *Free Space*." He eyed the small boat. "Want to try to make it to the nearest 7-Eleven in that one?"

"How long would it take?"

"Oh, seven or eight hours if we don't get lost."

For a moment she seriously considered the preposterous idea. "I'm not that desperate."

"I am. Let's radio for a plane to pick us up."

He started for the house, but she stopped him. "Wick, we can't give up now. Let's try to hold out a little longer."

He lifted her chin and searched her face. "Honey, it's bad enough for me—I feel like my guts have backlashed—but I know that you're hurting too. I can't take that. Let's call the plane."

"I'm okay," she said, a bit too brightly. Then a thought struck her, and she grabbed his hand. "Come with me." She hurried toward the house with Wick in tow. "I'm going to hypnotize you."

"But what about your ethics?"

"There are times when a situation transcends the usual rules. This is one of them."

A few minutes later they were in the living room with Wick stretched out on a striped cotton chaise.

"As I recall, you seemed susceptible to hypnosis in that introductory session at Fairmont Oil."

"I was. At first I felt as if my eyes were glued shut, just as you said." He grinned. "It was later that I had problems." He told her of his fantasy with her on the beach.

She gave him a playful swat. "This time I'll use another image. Close your eyes and take a deep breath."

"Are you sure this is going to work?"

"Certainly. Now, imagine yourself lying on a soft, fluffy cloud. You're floating, weightless and relaxed. You can feel the sun on your face, and a gently, warm breeze brushes your body. You feel so good and so relaxed . . . lying on a soft, fluffy cloud. With every breath you take, you go deeper and deeper into very relaxed feelings. So good and so relaxed . . . soft, fluffy cloud . . ."

She led him through the induction and, after making sure he was under, gave him several suggestions designed to relieve tension and make his craving disappear.

"Any time," she crooned to him, "that you find yourself becoming tense, all you have to do is say the word 'marshmallow' and your tension will vanish, as if by magic. And the next time I hypnotize you, all I'll have to do is ask you to close your eyes, count to seven, and you'll be back in a very relaxed state." She added her usual concluding statements. "One . . . two . . . three . . . four . . . five. Wide awake feeling great."

He opened his eyes, blinked, and smiled at her. "How do you feel?"

He stretched his arms. "Great. Human again."

"Do you want a cigarette?"

His brows drew together. "No, not particularly." He laughed. "Babe, you're fantastic!" He pulled her down on the chaise beside him and kissed her. "Thanks, sweetheart. You straightened me out quicker than Laura Bergstrom did."

"And who, may I ask, is Laura Bergstrom?"

He laughed and kissed her again. "She was the

great love of my life when I was sixteen. I was hell-bent on destruction, and Laura was a school counselor who personally barred the door and made me shape up. She convinced me that I was wasting my life goofing off and was smart enough to go to college."

"Another *older* woman, hum? Is this a pattern?"

He nibbled her lower lip. "She had about fifteen years on me. I was devastated when she married an insurance salesman before I could grow a mustache, declare my undying love, and propose to her. The first time I saw you, you reminded me a little of her. Not so much in looks—she had black hair and blue eyes—but something about your personality."

Perhaps it was silly, but Maya felt slightly indignant. "Gee, thanks. Now I discover I'm a substitute for your adolescent infatuation." She started to rise, but he held her.

"No, babe. You outclass her in every category. You're not a substitute for anything." His hand slid over the curve of her bottom, and his tongue teased the crease of her lips. "Besides," he said, devilment dancing in his expression, "she was just a wee bit cross-eyed."

Wick could hardly believe it, but he honestly didn't want a cigarette. And he couldn't remember when he'd felt so good. He was completely relaxed, but his mind was clear and sharp. The day seemed sunnier, colors seemed brighter, and his lady was the most beautiful, desirable woman in the world. Lord, how he loved her.

He felt closer to her than he'd ever felt before, as if they were becoming one. But he knew if he tried to explain it to her right now, she'd probably give him another psychological explanation about hypnosis and suggestibility and the powerful close attachment that can sometimes develop between hypnotist and subject. Transference, she'd called it, but he didn't buy that Freudian claptrap for a minute. He'd loved her even before they'd set foot on Crescent Cay, been under her spell from the first moment he saw her. Hypnosis hadn't changed that. The closeness was developing because they were spending more time together; his love was growing because each day he found her more lovable. As he sliced grapefruit he looked over at her and winked.

They were halfway through breakfast before it dawned on him. His forkful of eggs stopped before it reached his mouth. He'd been so caught up in the magic Maya had performed that he'd forgotten she was still in the same kind of hell he'd been in before she hypnotized him. He laid his hand over hers.

"Honey, you've cured me, but what are we going to do about you?"

Nine

Maya lay stretched out on the chaise. "I'm not sure this is going to work," she told Wick.

He dragged a chair close to her. "Now, love, that's no way to talk. You have to think positively. Of course it's going to work." He held up the yellow pad with the script she'd written for him. "I have explicit directions from the best hypnotist I know. You did it for me; now I'm going to do it for you."

Since she'd hypnotized Wick the day before, he'd been very solicitous of her and as happy as a clam. She'd become crosser than a crab. Her body was one big mass of writhing, raw nerve endings. Her ear hurt from wiggling the accursed staple; her jaws were sore from chewing that blasted gum; she'd eaten over half the coconut cake and two boxes of cookies by herself. And she was thinking seriously of rolling tea leaves in toilet paper and smoking them.

"Maybe we should just call for the plane," she suggested.

He squeezed her hand. "Let's give this a try first, honey."

"But my own self-hypnosis tapes never did me any good."

"Maybe that was because it was your own voice. If I make the suggestions, it'll be different. Do you trust me?"

"Yes, but—"

He silenced her with a kiss. "It *will* work."

It will *work*, she repeated to herself several times.

"Now lie back, close your eyes, and focus on your toes. Bend and tighten them. Tighter . . . tighter . . . hold it. Now relax, and let them go. You can feel warm, soothing, relaxing energy seeping into your toes."

She concentrated on the mellow timbre of his voice and followed his directions as he moved through the systematic process of contacting and relaxing every muscle group from her feet to her head. As she listened tension melted away and her body felt as if it were floating on a cloud. Lethargic, peaceful, receptive. She allowed his suggestions to wash over and through her. She wanted nothing more than to please him. Her wishes were his wishes.

His words were a resonant whisper coaxing her deeper and deeper into relaxed feelings. She felt *so* good and *so* relaxed. Boneless. Tranquilly she followed his lead until she was totally serene, weightless, malleable. When the gentle rumble of his voice ambled through her mind and reshaped her cravings, she offered no resistance, for his desires were her desires. They were one.

Floating on a cloud with soft sunshine warming her body felt wonderful, so wonderful that she was loath to leave the enchanted spot. But his voice was leading her back to wakefulness. Dreamlike, she followed his gentle bidding.

". . . four . . . five. Wide awake."

She opened her eyes, smiled and stretched.

"How do you feel?"

"Terrific. I haven't been so relaxed in ages." She stretched again and smiled at the dear, dear face watching her so intently.

"Want a cigarette?"

Frowning, she mentally searched her body and her thoughts. "No, I don't think so."

A broad grin broke over his face. "By damn, it worked! Pat Collins, move over. I may take my show on the road."

She laughed. "Don't get too carried away with yourself, Svengali. Hypnotizing someone is easy; it's knowing what to do when they're under that takes training. It's not a parlor game. Remember what I explained about lingering suggestibility and the unusual relationship that can—"

He bent and kissed her. "Okay, okay, Dr. Stephens. I get the message. But I was pretty good at it, wasn't I?" He gave her a smug grin.

Her arms lazily encircled his neck. "Very good. I was a better subject with you than I've ever been with anyone. It's your natural seductive nature."

He rubbed his nose against hers. "Seductive, am I?"

"Mmmm. Very. Did I ever tell you that you have eyes like a tiger?"

Chuckling, he growled and nipped at her throat. "Better to see you with, my dear."

"That's a wolf's line, not a tiger's." She laughed and held him close, feeling profoundly content and connected with him, basking in the afterglow of the melding of minds, savoring his smell, his warmth, his heartbeat. A small voice from her professional persona reminded her that she might merely be experiencing transference; the woman in her ignored the warning.

Giving her a quick kiss, he pulled away. "Are you up to some diving?" She nodded and he tugged her to her feet. "Let's go find those lobsters I promised you for lunch."

They gathered their diving gear and walked down to the end of the pier where a small coral reef lay an easy swim away. She felt light and carefree and wonderfully alive. After they slithered into yellow wet suits and fins, Wick helped her buckle on her tank. Equipment in place, they slid into the water and made for the reef.

In the warm turquoise water, schools of tiny silver fish darted through undulating sea plants, and a queen angelfish waved delicately only inches from Maya's mask. She reached her hand to it, and it fluttered away. Vivid-hued parrot fish fed among the new generation of coral, spectacularly colored and clinging to crusty boulders that were the tombs of its ancestors.

Only the sound of bubbles from their air tanks marred the awesome quiet of the underwater fantasy as they moved through the irregular formations searching for their prey.

Wick touched her shoulder and pointed to a ledge. They moved closer, and he picked up a large lobster before it could scuttle away. He deposited it in the mesh bag at his waist and motioned for her to get one. She shook her head slowly and pointed to him, then back to the ledge. His eyes crinkled behind his mask, and he pointed to her again, making it clear that she was responsible for her own lunch. Gingerly she picked up the wiggling crustacean and held it out for him to bag. Together they swam back toward the cay.

Back on the sandy beach they started stripping off their gear. "You rat," Maya said, skinning off her wet suit. "That lobster could have pinched my fingers off."

He laughed. "Not likely. Look at their smaller claws. These are different from New England varieties." He held one up before he dropped it into a bucket of seawater. "Down here things are made for loving, not fighting."

"Likely story."

She took two bottles of beer from the cooler and handed him one. He took a big swig, and, while he was toweling off, she took the bucket to the shade of a palm tree and knelt down beside it to examine their catch. He was right. The lobster's pinchers looked much less ominous than those she saw in the supermarket tanks.

Rising, she brushed the sand from her knees and turned toward him. He was stretched out on the white sand, his eyes closed and the beer bottle resting on his taut abdomen. Sunlight glinted off the fine blond hair on his arms and legs and shimmered it like gold. As her gaze traveled the tanned, muscled length of him desire rose within her like a living, breathing thing. It grew and swelled her chest until she was almost smothering with want of him. She wanted to run her tongue over every inch of him from toes to breeze-ruffled hair. Remembering his account of the beach fantasy he'd had during that first session at Fairmont Oil, she smiled.

* * *

Wick startled from his half-doze when the bottle was lifted from his hands. Maya, wearing nothing but sunlight and a siren's smile, knelt beside him. Her hair, tossed and dried by the wind, was copper fire around her shoulders, and her eyes were sea-green and heavy lidded.

She leaned over him, and he could feel the warmth of her breath on his belly, then her lips as they grazed the skin around his navel. His hands moved to slide over her full, creamy breasts and along the curve of her bare hip, but she captured them.

"Don't move," she whispered. "Just lie there and let me do this."

She tugged off his trunks and wove a wondrous spell of erotic teasing with lips and tongue from his toes to his forehead. She covered his mouth with hers and their tongues met. He groaned and his arms snaked around her.

"Ah-ah." She pulled away and gave him a sultry smile. "In this fantasy, only I can touch."

Her palms rubbed over his chest with long, slow strokes, and her auburn hair swept across his skin as she bent to nibble at his ear and whisper love words. She wove magic with sibilant sounds and languid touch until he was on fire with wanting her. There wasn't a part of him that she didn't brand with her mouth and tongue. Sweat popped out on his forehead and upper lip.

"I may not survive this," he gasped. "Babe, let me touch you."

She laughed. "Just relax." Her hand slid to the juncture of his thighs.

He jerked. "Relax, hell! Woman, are you crazy?"

Giving another low, throaty laugh, she straddled him with her long legs and began to lower herself on him. Her warmth encased him, and he strained toward her. She arched her back and rotated her hips as he slid deeper and deeper into her tight, wet heat.

"Oh, Lord, I love you," he groaned. His hands curled into fists as she circled and stroked him. "Come, let me taste your breasts."

She leaned forward until her nipple grazed his waiting mouth, and his lips closed around the tight bud and suckled. With a little whimper she pulled away and offered him the other.

His fantasy was forgotten; reality became hot and frantic and his hands were all over her. Their joining became a wild ride of grinding undulations and straining thrusts beneath a tropical sun until she flung back her head and arched with a breathless cry. Her rhythmic spasms hit him like shock waves, yanking him over the edge, ripping great gushing pulsations from his core. He gave a groaning shout of agonized pleasure and lay tensed until the last potent sensation was spent.

Still astride him, she leaned back against his bent knees. Her eyes were closed and a fine sheen of perspiration made her skin glow like satin. Her beautiful breasts rose and fell with shallow panting, and his fingers moved to circle their softness and touch the wetness his mouth had made. Love for her swelled in him until he was about to burst with it.

"I love you, Maya. I love you more than I ever thought it was possible to love a woman. Marry me."

Her eyes flew open, and he didn't like the look he saw in those green depths. She glanced away and tried to move. He gripped her waist and held her fast.

"Maya, look at me." Her eyes met his. "I love you. And unless you're a damned good actress, I think you care about me."

"Of course I care about you, Wick."

"Do you love me?" Tension knotted his belly.

Her eyes shimmered, and a tear slipped from one and rolled down her cheek. She pressed her lips together and nodded. Then tension uncoiled, and he let out the breath he didn't know he'd been holding.

"Babe, you scared me there for a minute." He wrapped his arms around her and pulled her down against his chest.

They lay there quietly as the waves lapped the white sand and canaries sang in the tamarind trees. He felt himself grow hard again, and he rolled her over and made love to her again. Slow, gentle, sweet love to his woman. His.

Maya couldn't sleep. She eased out of Wick's arms and slipped through the French doors that led to the balcony. The night breeze cooled her warm, bare skin, and she almost laughed when she realized she was naked. How comfortable she'd become with her nudity around Wick since she'd discovered her figure flaws were much more important to her than him. In fact, her body was browner and leaner from sun and exercise.

How dear he was, and how fiercely she loved him. She'd been dismayed to discover that despite her intentions, love had somehow crept in. Perhaps her feelings were mixed up with tropical islands and a bizarre transference/countertransference relationship due to their hypnosis sessions, but it felt like love. And love complicated things. She hadn't planned on falling in love. At least he hadn't mentioned marriage again since that day on the beach. Even though she gloried in their being lovers for now, marriage was out of the question. And because she accepted that affairs didn't last forever, a bitter-sweet melancholy stole over her.

A pair of strong arms circled her waist. Soft lips murmured against her ear. "I missed you."

"I couldn't sleep. I suppose I was dreading leaving tomorrow."

"We can stay longer if you'd like. Bingo won't be back for a month or two."

She shook her head. "I have a practice, remember? And you have a business to run. We have to return to the real world."

"We can come back here in a few months. Sooner even, if you want to spend our honeymoon here. I'd kind of been thinking about the Alps, but—" She stiffened in his arms. "Babe"—he turned her to face him—"what's wrong?" Moonlight reflected from his eyes, narrowed and searching hers.

"Wick, I can't marry you."

"Why in the hell not? I love you; you love me. We get along great together. Makes sense that we should get married."

"There are at least a half-dozen reasons why marriage is impossible."

"I can't think of one. Let's hear yours."

"Well, for one thing, I'm older than you."

He gave a disgusted snort. "Three years? That's nothing. That's the craziest thing I've ever heard. I wouldn't care if you were twenty years older. Fifty years older. I love *you*, babe, *you*."

"But I've already had my family. My son is in college. You need a younger wife who can give you children of your own."

"Let me pick my own wife." He kissed her on the nose. "And I pick you. What's the next reason?"

She shivered, less from the night air than from old memory tapes rising up to haunt her.

"You're getting chilled. Let's go inside and get you a robe."

Because it was easier to acquiesce than to deal with haunting memories, she agreed. Unfortunately, he wasn't content to discontinue their conversation even though she urged him to do so. Not even a passionate kiss deterred him. He turned on the lamp, wrapped her in a robe, and pulled her down onto his lap, determined to talk.

"Age and children are problems that we can deal with easily," he declared. "What are your other four reasons?"

"Are you forgetting about transference?"

"Sounded like bull to me."

She sighed and rolled her eyes heavenward. "Wick, you didn't even try to understand."

"Then explain it to me again."

"Freud first used the term, but all psychologists encounter it every day. It's a very real phenomenon, one of the basic concepts that is drummed into therapists in training. Simply put, patients often transfer strong bonds of positive or negative emotion from past relationships onto the therapist. They may react as if the therapist is a former lover, a special friend, or someone older, like a nurturing mother or an overprotective father *or* a high school counselor. In other words, it's a temporary reexperiencing of repressed emotions. Your original crush on Laura Bergstrom was a type of transference. Patients frequently imagine themselves in love with their therapists, and, occasionally, vice versa—countertransference. Sometimes the same thing happens with hypnotist and subject, but it isn't a real, lasting emotion."

Stroking his mustache with his thumb and index finer, he was quiet for a moment. Raising one eyebrow, he squinted at her. "Do you honestly believe that because you hypnotized me that I have you mixed up with my mother or a guidance counselor I haven't thought of in years?" He gave her a lascivious grin. "Babe, my mother never turned me on like you do."

"Oh, Wick!" In exasperation she slapped his shoulder with the heel of her hand. "You don't even try to understand." She tried to get up, but, laughing, he corralled her in his arms.

"Honey, I'm sorry, but I don't buy it. I think you're dancing around what's really bothering you, spouting psychological mumbo jumbo and thinking up excuses not to marry me. Give me the real reason, the big gun you're saving for the finale."

She hesitated. "I suppose it boils down to a matter of lifestyle. You're the adventurous type and I'm much more . . . reserved."

He let out a whoop of laughter. "You? Reserved? Tell me another one."

Anger flashed through her. She broke away, stood up, and glared at him. "All right! It's those *damned* helicopters you zip around in. I'm not going to get tied up with someone else who's going to get himself killed in one of those death traps! Never again!" She fled to the bathroom and slammed the door.

Leaning against the door while he rapped and called her name, she felt like such a ninny. Here she was a forty-year-old woman, a licensed psychologist who advocated communication as a problem solver, hiding in the bathroom like a recalcitrant child. What was it about Wick that unearthed all her secrets, brought out her worst characteristics and her hidden flaws? She'd been a reasonably well-adjusted person with her life firmly under control until she met him.

She opened the door. He stood waiting for her, one hand propped on the jamb, the other on his hip.

"I think we should talk about this," he said.

Some of her humor returned. "That's usually my line. But you're right."

They got into bed, and she snuggled against his shoulder. He wrapped his arms around her and held her close, waiting, she knew, for her to explain her outburst. She searched for the right words, saying at last only, "I lost one husband in a helicopter. You know how terrified I am of those things. I couldn't bear to go through it again."

He stroked her and kissed her forehead gently. "Honey, nothing is going to happen to me. I do more paperwork than flying these days, and when I do fly, I'm a careful pilot. Maybe I was a hotdogger in my younger days, but I've settled down. I don't take unnecessary chances like some of those guys had to do during the war. Why, with the superior equipment we have nowadays, if you know what you're doing, there's not much that can go wrong. Driving on the Houston freeways is more dangerous than flying a helicopter."

By the time he finished quoting statistics in his low, soothing voice, he almost had her convinced that her fears were groundless. Almost.

He brushed back her hair and kissed her temple. "I still want us to get married, but we'll just give it a little time, babe. I won't rush you or push you. Since we've met, I'm learning to be a patient man."

* * *

After three weeks back home things had settled into their usual routine. True to his word, Wick hadn't mentioned marriage again, but he'd professed his love, often. He'd even taken her on a tour of his offices and the hangar where the helicopters were kept. She'd decided that the machines were beginning to seem less ominous than they had before. And his pilots—although they were a flirtatious, gregarious bunch who were probably ordered to be on their best behavior with her around—seemed to be a sensible and competent group. He even employed one woman pilot who was married and the mother of a two-year-old.

While she was becoming somewhat less leery of his occupation, she was still far from comfortable with it and simply put it out of her mind as much as possible. Perhaps it was denial, but it enabled her to cope with the situation. After all, she had no intentions of marrying someone like Wick McCall. She made herself content with the idea of a temporary love affair and refused to think beyond the present.

The two of them had spent almost every free moment together until business had called Wick out of town.

"I hate to go, babe," he'd said. "But it's something I committed to several months ago. Nothing to worry about. Just a few days in Dallas. Strictly routine. I'll be back Saturday."

"I understand," she'd said when she kissed him good-bye. "Business is business. I'll miss you."

And she did miss him.

Friday night was dreary. It had rained for two days, rivers and bayous were full, some streets were flooded, and a series of storms moving in from the Gulf promised more of the same drenching weather for the weekend. Maya and Chelsea had decided to put on their fleecy robes, make a big bowl of popcorn, and watch movies on television.

Chelsea was checking the *TV Guide*, and Maya was digging out the popcorn popper when there was a tapping on the kitchen door. When Maya opened it, she found 'Fessor, water dripping from his floppy rain hat, holding a cat carrier covered with plastic and a bag of cat litter and food. From inside the carrier John Keats made disparaging noises about the indignity of his predicament.

"Come in, 'Fessor," Maya said. "You look as if you need a cup of tea. How about Red Zinger with lemon?"

"It's very tempting, my dear, but I don't want to track up your kitchen, and I still have to pack." He set the carrier down and leaned the bag against a cabinet. "Are you sure that John Keats won't be an imposition?"

"Not at all. You enjoy your bridge tournament."

He gave a merry chuckle. "I have every intention of trouncing my opponents and earning a few more master's points." He pulled a ring of keys from his pocket. "These are an extra set for you. This gold one is for the front door, the green for the back, the silver for the garage, and the blue one is to the river house." He gave her a playful wink. "You and your young man might like to spend the weekend at the river house. It's very cozy and private."

She laughed. "Thanks, 'Fessor, but we'll probably stay in town since the weather is so nasty."

"I like your Mr. McCall. I think he's just the man for you. Spirited, strong. Seems very fond of you."

"I'm fond of him, too."

"Forgive an old man's impertinence for asking, but might I hope to hear the peal of wedding bells soon?"

"Oh, I don't think so. We have some problems, I'm afraid."

"Nothing insurmountable, I hope. It would bring me great joy to see you happily settled with a loving mate."

"I appreciate your concern, but some things simply aren't meant to be." She kissed his wrinkled cheek, and with a final assurance that John Keats was no bother, she waved good-bye to the old gentleman.

When the door was closed, she let the Abyssinian out of his carrier, and he sauntered by, nose up and tail swishing, as if to remind her that such treatment was beneath his station. She laughed and dumped the oil and popcorn into the cooker.

Soon the kitchen filled with the savory scent of popcorn as kernels exploded in sizzling oil. The odor never failed to comfort her on a dreary night and set the mood for a good movie. She wished that Wick were here to share it. She was pouring the delicious-smelling stuff into a bowl when Chelsea shrieked and screamed for her to come quickly.

Heart pounding, Maya ran to the den.

"Look, look," Chelsea said, pointing to the TV.

There, in living color, Wick's grinning face filled the screen.

"Hollywood has come to Dallas," the woman reporter said, "and the handsome hunk, Wick McCall of Houston, is one of the stunt pilots for what director Robert Weldon promises is the most exciting helicopter chase scene ever filmed. Streets were closed for two hours yesterday as hundreds

of downtown office workers witnessed the shoot-
ing of *Hot Moon*, starring Sean Ellison and Wendy
Morris. Here are some electrifying clips from yesterday's action."

Maya stood frozen as she watched two helicopters, one red, one blue-and-white, zoom between
skyscrapers, flying so low that the skids almost
creased the tops of cars. Men hanging out of the
open cockpits fired machine guns at one another
as the two crafts engaged in a reckless pursuit.

Horrified, bile rising in her throat, she saw the
choppers rise, then drop, streaking through city
streets in a mad chase. They darted around corners of buildings, cutting in so close that the
whirling blades nearly sliced the masonry. A bar-
rage of bullets ripped through the tail section of
the blue-and-white and threw sparks from its rotors. Smoke coughed and poured from the engine. It sputtered, whined, and lurched back and
forth, up and down in a frenzied struggle to avoid
smashing against the sides of the unyielding ur-
ban canyon. A close-up from the cockpit of the
damaged helicopter zoomed in on their distorted
reflection as they careened toward certain obliv-
ion against a shimmering glass and steel butte.
Closer and closer and closer. Then the screen exploded into a billowing orange fireball.

Maya screamed, dropped to her knees, and covered her face.

Ten

It wasn't real, she told herself. *It wasn't real.* But the horror of what she'd witnessed clung to her. Watching the film clip on TV and knowing that Wick was flying the blue-and-white helicopter had ripped out and exposed her deepest, most paralyzing fears.

Chelsea tried to comfort her, but she was beyond consolation. She went for a walk; she tried to read; she paced the floor and tried to reason with herself. Nothing worked. Her brain continued its charge, frenetic and surrealistic, flashing disconnected scenes like blips from the window of a runaway express train. She couldn't seem to escape or control her thoughts. It was like trying to gather an armload of agitated bees.

By Saturday morning Maya was physically and emotionally exhausted, wrung out. She'd slept in only fitful snatches between nightmares that replayed helicopter crashes, blood, flames, and screams. In her mind, fantasy and reality, Vietnam and Dallas, skyscrapers and forested hill,

Wick and Ron, were a terrifying amalgam that haunted her sleep and tormented her wakefulness.

At dawn she'd given up any pretense at sleep. She'd drunk coffee and paced, listening to the gray rain pelt against the windows. Chelsea had tried to talk to her, but Maya was in no mood for talk as she grappled in hand-to-hand combat with the demons of her mind. She smiled, assuring Chelsea that she was okay and was relieved when her sister-in-law left for her study group meeting.

As the morning wore on, her anxiety burgeoned into a twisted Hydra of horror, revulsion, and rage. It was if the emotions she'd experienced and thought she'd dealt with at the time of Ron's death had resurfaced a hundredfold. Her worst fears had come upon her, and she railed at her idiocy in getting involved with someone like Wick. What she'd witnessed on the screen wasn't merely a fantasy, it was a portend of a future with Wick McCall. Damn him!

The more she replayed the situation, the more her fury whipped its barbed tail. By the time the telephone rang, her outrage was white-hot. She snapped a terse, "Hello."

"Good morning, babe. Have you missed me? I have a flight out of Dallas in about fifteen minutes. Can you pick me up at the airport in Houston?"

"When hell freezes over!" She slammed down the phone.

In less than a minute it started ringing again. She ignored it. It continued its shrill demand. Still seething, she jerked it up.

"Honey, it's me, Wick. What's going on?"

"Your hotdogging days are over, huh? Nothing

to worry about, you said. Strictly routine." Sarcasm dripped from her words. "Toad! Liar!"

"Maya, what the hell are you talking about?"

"I know all about your *routine* business. They had a film clip from *Hot Moon* on TV, with you in living color. It's bad enough that you're fool enough to do such a dangerous thing; it's worse to lie about it."

"Oh, babe." He laughed. "That was nothing. A bunch of movie tricks."

Her fury accelerated to an explosive intensity. "Don't you dare laugh, you overgrown exhibitionist! How *could* you, Wick? Do you have any idea what torment I've endured since last night? I must have been mad to get mixed up with somebody like you again!"

"Maya, honey, they're calling my flight. I'll be at your house in two hours. We'll talk about this then."

"Don't you dare come here. We're finished. I don't want to see or hear of you again. Ever."

"Babe, be reasonable. I—"

She slammed down the receiver and dropped her forehead in her hand. That man had reduced her to screaming like a shrew, and she *never* screamed or had bad-tempered fits. Before she'd met Wick, she'd always been in perfect control. Perhaps she was behaving like a child in a tantrum, but she didn't care. Only her fury was powerful enough to overcome the gut-wrenching horror and despair that had plagued her. Anger felt good. Damned good.

Thank Heaven she hadn't agreed to marry him. Wick McCall could kill himself playing daredevil in one of those stupid helicopters if he wanted to, but she didn't intend to be around to have to grieve for him. Things had to end sometime; it might as well be now before she was any more deeply invested. Perhaps this incident was a blessing in disguise. Their flaming love affair was over. Accepting the fact, she wrestled for control and began to replace the restraining wall against her turbulent feelings, brick by brick.

"Joy-jockey jerk," she muttered.

John Keats twined around her legs and meowed his agreement.

For her own emotional sanity she never wanted to see Wick again. But if she knew him, and she did, he'd be banging on her door by noon. She wouldn't be around to listen. She didn't want to talk to him; her emotions were still too raw, too fragile. Perhaps in a few days they could have a rational discussion and end their relationship amicably, but not now.

Searching her mind for an appropriate place of refuge, she discarded the idea of a hotel or motel. Since Chelsea wouldn't be home until the wee hours, she had to consider John Keats, and she didn't relish being cooped up in a room with a cat for the weekend. Her eye caught the multicolored keys on the kitchen counter. 'Fessor's river house. Perfect.

After throwing a few things in a bag and scribbling a note to Chelsea—with a stern admonition not to reveal her destination to Wick—Maya coaxed John Keats into his carrier. He raised a ruckus, but she ignored him, and donned her rain gear. In two trips she'd loaded everything into her car, locked the house, and sloshed back to the garage. The backyard looked like a rice paddy, and water poured from the dark sky in great torrents.

When she backed out of the garage, rain struck

the fabric top of the Mustang with a hollow thumping like hailstones against a canvas tent. She briefly considered the difficulty of getting out in such weather, but she ignored the niggling concern and shut the door with her automatic unit. On the street, water washed curb-high as she drove slowly through the flood-prone city. Avoiding routes that, as a long time resident, she knew were often underwater during a heavy deluge, she made her way to the freeway and headed away from the city.

Even with the wipers clacking at high speed, she had to lean forward and peer through the gray sheets of blowing rain. John Keats yowled from the backseat and clawed at the door of his cage.

"Calm down, old fellow," she said. "We'll be there soon, and you can get out."

John Keats wasn't mollified. The level of his caterwauling increased until her frayed nerves were threadbare and her fingers hurt from her death grip on the steering wheel. She turned on the radio to drown him out.

". . . another wide band of heavy thunderstorms with potentially damaging winds is moving in from the Gulf. A travel advisory urges motorists to stay off the streets and highways unless travel is absolutely necessary."

"*Now* you tell me," she said to the radio as she turned off onto the road leading to the river house.

"The following streets and underpasses are closed due to high water." The announcer droned on with the list, then added, "Officials have expressed their concern over the high level of Lake Houston and have announced that they may have to release water into the San Jacinto River if the level continues to rise in the next several hours. Residents along the San Jacinto should stay tuned for further bulletins and be prepared to evacuate. And now for music to stay in and roast marshmallows by."

"Great, just great." 'Fessor's house was on the bank of the San Jacinto River, downstream from the dam.

Lena Horne's rendition of *Stormy Weather* mixed with the yowls in the back as Maya strained to see the edge of black asphalt. Should she go back home? She took the left fork of the winding road, drove another mile and a half, and pulled to a stop by the 'Fessor's redwood house on cedar pilings. Only a few yards away, the muddy river churned precariously high in its banks and flowed swiftly around the bend, a dead limb swept along in the roar.

"John Keats, the water has a long way to go before it will be dangerous, but I think it would be smart for us to find a hotel instead. What do you think?"

He howled.

"I agree."

She backed up to turn around and felt her rear tires sink into something soft. "Oh, please, no," she moaned. She eased the car forward, but the rear tires whined as they spun helplessly and slung mud. She tried rocking the car back and forth, but she only sunk deeper and deeper.

Cramming her rain hat on her head, she slogged through the downpour, gathered pine branches, and stuck them under the back. All she got for her trouble was a shoe full of mud, and water down her neck.

"I'll have to call the wrecker," she told the cat. "You stay here." When she started to get out, he screeched so loud that she relented. Draping plastic over his cage, she carried him with her.

Inside she peeled off her ruined sneakers and socks and dropped her raincoat and hat into a wet puddle beside them. Taking pity on the mewling cat, she opened the door to the carrier, and a brown streak shot across the room and lodged under the couch.

She turned on the lights and searched the cozy little house. It didn't take long because in addition to the living area, there were only two bedrooms, a bath, and a kitchen.

"We have a problem," she said to John Keats, who had come out from under the couch and was sitting on the hearth, looking at her reproachfully. "No phone. It looks like we're stuck here—no pun intended—whether we like it or not."

Wick rang the bell and banged on the door until his knuckles were raw. He let out a string of blasphemous oaths and trudged through the rain to the garage, not caring if water ran in his shoes and plastered his clothes to him. He couldn't get any wetter. Shielding his eyes with his hand, he peered through the garage window. Both spaces were empty. Damn.

He crossed the side yard and rang the bell at Dr. Newberry's front door. Nobody answered and the house looked dark. He tried the neighbors on the other side of Maya's house, and a woman there said she'd seen Chelsea leave earlier in the morning, but she didn't know about Maya. Inquiries at several other houses yielded no better results. Thoroughly drenched, with his hair plastered to his head and rivulets running from his chin, he got in the taxi waiting at the curb and went home.

Although the rain seemed to be slacking off, the trip to his apartment through a circuitous route of snarled traffic took almost three hours. Flooding was widespread. At several underpasses water covered the tops of cars driven by fools who didn't have enough sense to realize the damned things weren't boats. By the time he reached his house, he was imagining Maya trapped in high water somewhere, wet and frightened.

Before he stripped off his sodden clothes, he grabbed the phone and dialed her number. It rang twenty times before he cursed and slammed down the receiver. Where the hell was she? He called every friend and acquaintance of Maya's that he could think of and rang her number every few minutes for the next several hours, growing more alarmed and feeling more impotent with each futile attempt.

Damn that stupid movie and damn that stupid TV reporter who'd interviewed him in Dallas and damn his rotten luck that Maya had seen it! He raked his fingers through his hair and paced. He should have told her about the movie, but he'd known she'd overreact. Not that there was anything really dangerous about what he'd done, but he'd seen the clip. And with special effects, lots of smoke, and a zoom lens, he had to admit that it had looked scary. The stunt coordinator on the picture was an old friend of his, and Wick had promised months ago that he'd do the job. He'd gotten a kick out of it, and a nice piece of change for a couple days of work. How could he have been such an idiot? She was going to be even madder if he told her he had to go back to Dallas next week to reshoot a few scenes.

He snatched up the phone and tried again.

The rain and the whipping winds stopped just before dusk. Maya tried placing limbs and boards under the wheels of the Mustang for traction, but it wouldn't budge. She considered walking out, but the house was secluded and she had no idea how far the closest neighbor lived. With night fast approaching, she didn't dare start out without a sure destination. Her only other mode of transportation was an aluminum canoe stored under the house, but only a fool would put a canoe in the swift, muddy San Jacinto now. She wished for Wick, then stopped her thoughts. He was no longer a part of her life. She was on her own. But she was a strong, resourceful woman; she could take care of herself. At first light in the morning she would go for help.

She built a fire with dry logs from a generous supply stacked neatly and covered with a tarp on the back porch, then took a shower. After she dressed in a moss-colored velour sweat suit, warm socks, and dry sneakers, she settled on the couch to watch the evening news. John Keats jumped into her lap, and she stroked him absently, focusing on the reports.

The majority of the stories were about the weather and the havoc it had wrecked around the city. Some sections were without power and phone service, many events had been canceled, and hundreds of people were stranded in their cars. Ron Stone, the anchorman on Channel 2, announced that Lake Houston was still rising from runoff and that residents along the lower San Jacinto River had been asked to evacuate as a precautionary measure.

Maya's heart lurched, and she leaned forward, clutching John Keats in her lap. Just as they switched to a reporter interviewing a representative from the sheriff's office, the lights flickered. The screen and the room went dark. Only the flames from the fireplace provided illumination.

"Don't panic," she told the purring cat as her stroking accelerated. "It's a temporary power failure. And the floodgates haven't been opened yet. The evacuation is merely precautionary. Never mind that it's dark and there's probably not another living soul around for miles. We'll be just fine. We have a flashlight, a battery radio, plenty of food, and a supply of wood."

She lit a kerosene lamp and carried it to the kitchen. After she'd fed the cat, she heated a can of vegetable soup on the butane stove. As an afterthought, she drew up several containers of water while her tea steeped.

Maya stepped out onto the deck, sipped her chamomile, and strained her eyes toward the darkness. She couldn't see a thing. But the night was filled with the shrill cacophony of thousands of tree frogs and the rushing tumble of the swift river. Sharp scents of wet pine and mellower odors of sodden, rotting humus hung in the damp air. The Abyssinian wound around her legs and purred.

"It's really quite peaceful here. Nothing to worry about at all. Remember, I left a note for Chelsea, and she's sure to send someone looking for us tomorrow."

John Keats sat back on his haunches, cocked his head up at her, and meowed.

"I know it was stupid of me to go tearing out of the house like a madwoman to avoid Wick. Especially in such bad weather. But you can't imagine how distraught I was. Ordinarily I'd never do such an outrageous thing, but something about Wick McCall makes me behave totally out of character. What is it about him that creates such turmoil in me?"

The cat meowed again.

"I don't know either." She sipped her tea. "You don't happen to have a cigarette on you, do you?"

John Keats only looked at her and blinked.

They went back inside and prowled the house together.

Maybe it was her early Girl Scout training or maybe it was just to give her something to do to keep from falling into an exhausted sleep, but around midnight, Maya searched out a first aid kit and extra batteries. She stuffed them, along with a flashlight, a filet knife, a jar of peanut butter, a stack of crackers, a box of Fig Newtons, a canteen of water, several foil packets of cat food, and her wallet, into a waterproof backpack. For good measure she added matches, a nylon windbreaker, and two Milky Ways. There was a third candy bar in the pantry, but she ate it. She also ate a whole package of dried apricots and a can of smoked almonds while she sat on the couch with the Walkman over her ears, staring at the fire.

By three o'clock in the morning the carpet pile was packed along the trail Wick had paced. His hair had been combed a thousand times with his fingers, and the air was tinted with colorful maledictions and creative epithets. Still nobody answered the phone, and the police and highway department had closed all the routes between his house and hers. He knew because he'd tried to run one of the barricades an hour ago and had almost landed in the slammer.

He'd phoned Camilla and Chelsea three times each, left countless messages with Maya's office answering service, plus called all the hospitals, hotels, and motels in the city—even the ones with water beds and XXX-rated movies in the rooms— and Dr. Newberry still didn't answer his phone either. Where in the hell could she be?

Enough of this crap! He slammed out of his apartment, got in the Corvette, and peeled rubber for Hooks Airport.

A few minutes later he lifted off in a new police helicopter that one of his pilots had ferried in Saturday morning and was due for delivery Monday. As he flew over the city he could see the flashing lights of emergency vehicles, streetlights shimmering over houses surrounded by murky lakes, cars still half-submerged in deep water, and long lines of others pulled to a stop waiting for the flood to recede. He searched among them for a white convertible, but he knew spotting her would be a long shot.

He hovered over her house, looking for a light, praying that she was safe asleep in bed and too stubborn to answer her phone. There wasn't room to land in her yard, and the big oak trees extending over the street made it impossible to set down there. He fanned out, searching for a spot, and settled on the parking lot of a church two blocks away.

He jogged back to the dark house and rang the bell impatiently. When there was no answer, he went around back and checked the garage again. Empty. Totally frustrated, he stalked to the back door, knocked, and rattled the knob. Nothing. Why hadn't it occurred to him to get a key from Maya? She had a key to his apartment, but she'd never reciprocated. He looked at the multipaned glass in the back door, raked his fingers through his hair, and took a deep breath. What the hell? Things couldn't get much worse. He picked up a flower pot and smashed a pane. After a couple of extra licks to knock out jagged shards, he reached through and unlocked the door.

Turning on lights as he went, he searched the entire house. Maya's bed was a tangle of covers, but she wasn't in it. Chelsea's room was empty. The whole house was empty. He went back to the kitchen, started a pot of coffee, and sat down to wait. That's when he spotted the note on the table.

Chelsea—
John Keats and I have gone to 'Fessor's river house. *Do not*, on pain of death, tell Wick where I am. I want to be alone. Call you tomorrow.

M.

Wick clenched his teeth. "Lady, you're in for a surprise!" But where in the hell was the river house? He grabbed up the phone and called Dr. Newberry's number. Still no answer. He must be with Maya, and he meant to find them. He jumped up, stalked out, and started knocking on doors in the neighborhood.

At the third house he tried, a sleepy man in

striped pajamas rubbed his sparse tufts of gray hair and said, "I know that he bought a river place a few years ago, but I don't know the exact location. Maya Stephens would know."

Wick cursed silently and muttered a terse, "Thanks." He was about to try another neighbor when he saw Chelsea's car pull into the driveway. He sprinted across the street and met her at the back door.

"Wick! What's happened? The door's been smashed. Where's Maya? I've been calling and calling—"

"She's at Dr. Newberry's river house. Do you know where it is?"

"Sure, it's on the San Jacinto River."

"My Lord!" Wick exploded.

Eleven

Maya jolted awake as something landed on her chest. She was chilled, and John Keats' sharp claws dug into her skin. She could see by the dim flickering of the kerosene lamp that his back was arched, and he was hissing into her face. But there was no sound. She felt for the cushioned earphones still clamped over her head. The batteries must be dead, she thought, removing the earpieces. And the fire had gone out. A dank, fishy smell mixed with the odor of wet ashes.

"Sorry, old fellow. I must have stretched out on the couch and dropped off." She stroked the cat until he released his claw hold. "Are you cold? I'll start another fire."

When her foot touched the floor, it went ankle-deep in water. Her heart almost stopped. How long had she been asleep? She held her watch to the light. It was almost four-thirty. The last thing she remembered was the radio announcing one o'clock and playing a golden oldie. They must have opened the floodgates while she slept. She had to get to higher ground. But where? How?

Panic rose up, threatening to overwhelm her. "Stay calm," she cautioned herself. "Think."

She set the cat aside, got to her feet, and retrieved the big flashlight from the backpack she'd left on the coffee table. She waded to the front door and opened it. Aiming the light out into the darkness, she was horrified at what she saw. All around her swirled murky, yellowish-brown river. The house was an island, cut off from any escape by muddy water, at least six feet deep and—if it weren't her imagination—rising. The canoe was either submerged under the house's tall cedar pilings or was long gone.

Shrill *chirrs* of tree frogs and the deeper *ribbit-ribbit* of bull frogs echoed through the darkness, accented with an occasional plop and splash in the turbid water. She shone the light over the spot where she'd left her new convertible. Where it had been, a long, dark form slithered over the water's surface. Her skin crawled and she shuddered. Water moccasin. Probably hundreds of the slimy, poisonous things swam unseen among the submerged tree limbs. Before long they would be slithering through the house as the water rose. She shuddered again.

Higher. She had to get higher.

Holding onto the porch railing and leaning out, she searched with the beam of the flashlight for a way to climb onto the roof. The only tree close enough to the house was a tall pine with no low branches. She tried the other side and the back with no better results.

The water was two inches over her ankles. Right now she'd almost sell her soul for a ladder. 'Fessor was bound to have one, but it was probably the same place as the canoe. She swiped cold sweat from her face with her sleeve and fought to control her anxiety. Think. Think.

An idea came to her. The attic. Wood shingles. She could do it. Sloshing from room to room, she shone the light at the ceiling, looking for the access. She found the small square area on the inside corner of a bedroom. But there was no chain, no cord to pull it down.

She dragged a chest and a chair under the opening, climbed up, and slid away the piece of Sheetrock that fit over the square hole. Angling the beam of light upward, she decided her plan would work.

First, she took a quilt that was folded at the foot of the bed and stuffed it through the access, then went to the kitchen for a hammer, nails, and an old pair of work gloves. On her way back she stopped to retrieve the pack, and John Keats yowled, flung herself into her arms, and clung to the front of her shirt.

"We're going to be okay, fellow. Calm down. I'll put you in the attic first and come back for the other stuff."

A few moments later the water was almost midcalf as she pulled on a jacket and waded back with the paraphernalia. She tried not to think of snakes and other slimy creatures.

Inside the attic, which was really only an insulated crawl space, John Keats had curled up on the quilt and gone to sleep. "You're a trusting soul."

She set the lamp in a corner of the rafters and, picking a spot near the peak, Maya swung the hammer against the wooden shingles. She banged them again and again until she'd knocked a jagged hole in the roof.

"Sorry, John Keats, but I need your quilt."

The Abyssinian protested loudly as she rousted him from his bed, but she laughed and tossed the quilt through the hole and over the ridgepole of the roof.

"If I'm going to have to ride a roof, I plan to be as comfortable as possible." With a few long nails from her pocket, she secured the quilt to the ridgeboard, drove in a couple more nails partway, and looped a strap of the backpack over them. She stuck the flashlight and the hammer in a pocket of the pack, then shoved John Keats through the hole, blew out the lamp, and climbed up after him.

For the moment, her adrenaline was flowing and this all seemed like a grand adventure. Either the water would subside or someone would be along to rescue them in a few hours. They could hold out till then.

But gradually her breathing slowed and her wet feet grew chilled. She pulled one end of the quilt over her, and she and the cat sat huddled on the roof watching the moon's reflection on the dusky water and listening to the night sounds. She'd been so busy fighting for a way to survive, she hadn't had much time to think, but now that she'd done all she could, there was nothing to do but wait. And think.

What if the cedar pilings gave way? She and John Keats would be swept into that terrible, swirling river.

She opened the box of Fig Newtons and ate one. Then another. Was it her imagination or was the house beginning to sway?

Her imagination, surely.

She became very still, attuned to every sound and every movement of the wooden structure.

There was a very definite sway. A cold sweat popped out on her forehead, and for the first time she faced the fact that she could die here.

David.

He was coming home for Thanksgiving in a few days. She didn't want to die without seeing her son and telling him once more how much she loved him. Tears stung her eyes. If she died, David would be left with no parents at all. She hadn't had sense enough to think of danger and dying when she'd so stubbornly left home in the middle of a storm. Dying had never crossed her mind. She'd only done what she felt she must do at the time. Would David be angry that such a stupid and selfish act had led to her death? Would he be as furious with her as she'd been with Ron for—

Furious with Ron? Where had that come from? She hadn't been angry with Ron for dying. Grief-stricken, devastated to the depths of her soul, yes. But not angry. Never angry.

Or had she? From her perspective as a psychologist, she knew it was normal to be angry with a loved one for dying and leaving the survivor alone. Had she repressed her anger all these years? Surely not.

But the more she examined her psyche, the more convinced she was that she had a deep well of anger against Ron bottled up inside her. She tugged at the string of her unconscious until it unraveled. A geyser of fury poured from her, and she screamed with rage. John Keats bowed his back and hissed and spat along with her. Yes, she was angry. Bloody, blinding, bitterly *furious*.

Seventeen years. She had carried her repressed anger for seventeen years. Only the surface had healed. Below the scar tissue, a venomous sore had festered. She had relabeled her rage and called it fear. Poor Wick. He'd gotten the brunt of it.

Wick.

How she wished she could see him again. She would hold him and tell him she loved him. She'd worried so about his tempting danger, but it was she who was flirting with death. How stupid she'd been to let her fears come between them. Some time was better than no time. Life was too precious, too uncertain to waste a minute of it.

She sat with John Keats cuddled in her arms and told him about all the good times she and Wick had shared. Sometimes she smiled, and sometimes she laughed aloud. He purred and licked her face. She ripped open a packet of cat food and fed him the foul-smelling stuff bit by bit as she talked. When the package was empty, she wiped her hands on her damp pants, opened the box of Fig Newtons, and munched on them as she related stories of David when he was little.

The frogs cheeped and croaked, unseen things plopped and splashed in the water, and somewhere in the distance she heard a flutter. She tore open a Milky Way, talking to the cat between bites, and tried not to think about the swiftly flowing river that continued to rise. Or the sway of the roof they perched on.

The faint *whop-whopping* flutter grew louder, and she stilled, straining to hear the sound. Through the treetops came a brief flicker of light. A falling star? The lightning from another storm? She stopped chewing and concentrated on watching and listening. Another sweep of light, then another. The sound grew louder.

"It's a helicopter, John Keats! A helicopter. Oh, Lord, I've never heard anything so wonderful."

She threw down the candy bar and grabbed the flashlight. In her haste she fumbled it, and it went skittering down the roof. She made a grab for it and started sliding down the shingles. Catching hold of the quilt, she pulled herself back up, cursing her stupidity.

The sound of the rotors was closer and a spotlight swept the river ahead of it. She yelled and waved her arms, but she knew she couldn't be heard or seen. What if they missed her?

The lamp. She crawled back through the hole and felt around for the old kerosene light, wishing she'd left it burning, but she hadn't wanted to risk being roasted as well as drowned. Her fingers touched glass, then closed around the base. Holding it carefully, she hoisted herself back up through the hole. She lit the wick and replaced the chimney. The helicopter was coming closer, and she waved the lamp in a wide arc.

The beam of the spotlight found her, and as the chopper hovered overhead, she could see POLICE written on the fiberglass tail section. She blew out the lamp and lowered it back through the hole to the attic, then waved her arms.

"Maya Stephens?" a voice said over the loudspeaker.

"Yes!" she screamed and waved her arms.

"I'm coming down. If I get one skid on the roof, can you climb in?" the voice boomed.

"Yes!" She nodded vigorously. She was going to make it! Her feeling of elation must have been the same one dozens of wounded soldiers had felt when they heard the choppers coming in to rescue them. Silently she blessed Ron Stephens and the important work he did and let him go.

She emptied the backpack of all but her wallet

and put John Keats inside. Keeping the pack in front, she looped the straps around her shoulders, crouched against the roof, and held on to the quilt as the draft whipped her hair and clothes. The helicopter came closer and closer until one skid touched the roof only a few feet from where she stood.

"Open the door and get in."

She didn't have to be told twice. She grabbed the handle, opened the door, and scrambled inside by the pilot.

"Wick!"

He grinned. "You can't get away from me." His voice boomed over the loudspeaker. "Buckle up, babe. We're out of here."

She threw back her head and laughed, then reached for the belt. As the chopper lifted, the pack on her chest came alive. Poor John Keats. She unzipped the pocket enough for his head to poke through before she put on her earphones.

"I've never been so glad to see anyone in my life. How did you find me? John Keats and I were afraid we might have to swim for it. She giggled.

"There's not a damned thing funny about this! I've almost been out of my mind."

"Welcome to the club."

"As soon as I can set this thing down, I'm going to give you the tongue-lashing of your life. Right after I kiss you senseless."

He landed in the parking lot of a supermarket and did just that. She went into his arms gladly, reveling in his touch, returning his ardor.

John Keats sent up a howl as he was squashed between them. They laughed and drew apart.

"We'll continue this later," he said.

* * *

They lay in Wick's bed, snuggled close, luxuriating in the warm afterglow of lovemaking. He stroked the length of her arm, then kissed her damp forehead. "Honey, you scared the devil out of me. If you ever, *ever* pull a stunt like that again, I'm going to wring your beautiful neck."

"It was a dumb thing to do, I admit. But, speaking of stunts, why did you lie to me about the movie?"

"I didn't lie."

She raised up and gave him an exasperated look. "I saw you on television."

"I just skirted the truth a little. I was never in any danger, but I knew you'd be upset. And you were."

Very gently she explained about her fears and all the things she'd discovered about herself while she sat on the rooftop.

"All your old ghosts gone?" he asked.

"All gone." She snuggled back into his arms. "I love you, Wick. I love you more than I ever believed it was possible to love anyone."

"I love you, too, babe." He squeezed her, and they lay quietly, enjoying the warmth and closeness between them. "Hey, I just realized that you didn't come unglued when you were in the chopper."

"Nope."

"That's fantastic, honey. Does this mean that we can get married soon?"

"On one condition."

He cocked one wicked brow. "And that is?"

She laughed. "That you teach me to fly. I've discovered that I *love* helicopters."

THE EDITOR'S CORNER

It's a pleasure to return to the Editor's Corner while Susann Brailey is away on maternity leave, the proud mother of her first child—a beautiful, big, healthy daughter. It is truly holiday season here with this wonderful addition to our extended "family," and I'm delighted to share our feelings of blessings with you . . . in the form of wonderful books coming your way next month.

First, let me announce that what so many of you have written to me asking for will be in your stockings in just thirty days! Four classic LOVESWEPT romances from the spellbinding pen of Iris Johansen will go on sale in what we are calling the **JOHANSEN JUBILEE** reissues. These much-requested titles take you back to the very beginning of Iris's fabulous writing career with the first four romances she wrote, and they are **STORMY VOWS, TEMPEST AT SEA, THE RELUCTANT LARK,** and **BRONZED HAWK**. In these very first love stories published in the fall and winter of 1983, Iris began the tradition of continuing characters that has come to be commonplace in romance publishing. She is a true innovator, a great talent, and I'm sure you'll want to buy all these signed editions, if not for yourself, then for someone you care about. Could there be a better Christmas present than an introduction to the love stories of Iris Johansen? And look for great news inside each of the JOHANSEN JUBILEE editions about her captivating work coming in February, **THE WIND DANCER**. Bantam, too, has a glorious surprise that we will announce next month.

Give a big shout "hooray" now because Barbara Bowell is back! And back with a romance you've requested—**THE LAST BRADY,** LOVESWEPT

(continued)

#444. Delightful Colleen Brady gets her own romance with an irresistibly virile heartbreaker, Jack Blackledge. He's hard to handle—to put it mildly—and she's utterly inexperienced, so when he needs her to persuade his mother he's involved with a nice girl for a change, the sparks really fly. As always, Barbara Boswell gives you a sweet, charged, absolutely unforgettable love story.

A hurricane hits in the opening pages of Charlotte Hughes's **LOUISIANA LOVIN'**, LOVESWEPT #445, and its force spins Gator Landry and Michelle Thurston into a breathlessly passionate love story. They'd been apart for years, but how could Michelle forget the wild Cajun boy who'd awakened her with sizzling kisses when she was a teenager? And what was she to do with him now, when they were trapped together on Lizard Bayou during the tempest? Fire and frenzy and storm weld them together, but insecurity and pain threaten to tear them apart. A marvelous LOVESWEPT from a very gifted author!

SWEET MISCHIEF, LOVESWEPT #446, by Doris Parmett is a sheer delight. Full of fun, fast-paced, and taut with sexual tension, **SWEET MISCHIEF** tells the love story of sassy Katie Reynolds and irresistible Bill Logan. Bill is disillusioned about the institution of marriage and comes home to his childhood friend Katie with an outrageous proposition. . . . But Katie has loved him long enough and hard enough to dare anything, break any rules to get him for keeps. Ecstasy and deep emotion throw Bill for a loop . . . and Katie is swinging the lasso. **SWEET MISCHIEF** makes for grand reading, indeed. A real keeper.

Bewitching is the first word that comes to mind to
(continued)

describe Linda Cajio's LOVESWEPT #447, **NIGHTS IN WHITE SATIN**. When Jill Daneforth arrives in England determined to get revenge for the theft of her mother's legacy, she is totally unprepared for Rick Kitteridge, an aristocrat and a devil of temptation. He pursues her with fierce passion—but an underlying fear that she can never be wholly his, never share more than his wild and wonderful embraces. How this tempestuous pair reconciles their differences provides some of the most exciting reading ever!

Witty and wonderful, **SQUEEZE PLAY,** LOVESWEPT #448, from beloved Lori Copeland provides chuckles and warmth galore. As spontaneous as she is beautiful, Carly Winters has to struggle to manage her attraction to Dex Mathews, the brilliant and gorgeous ex-fiance who has returned to town to plague her in every way . . . including competing in the company softball game. They'd broken up before because of her insecurity over their differences in everything except passion. Now he's back kissing her until she melts, vowing he loves her as she is . . . and giving you unbeatable romance reading.

Sweeping you into a whirlwind of sensual romance, **LORD OF LIGHTNING,** LOVESWEPT #449, is from the extraordinary writer, Suzanne Forster. Lise Anderson takes one look at Stephen Gage and knows she has encountered the flesh-and-blood embodiment of her fantasy lover. As attracted to her as she is to him, Stephen somehow knows that Lise yearns to surrender to thrilling seduction, to abandon all restraint. And he knows, too, that he is just the man to make her dreams come true. But her fears collide with his . . . even as they show

(continued)

each other the way to heaven . . . and only a powerful love can overcome the schism between this fiercely independent schoolteacher and mysterious geologist. **LORD OF LIGHTNING**—as thrilling a romance as you'll ever hope to read.

Six great romances next month . . . four great Iris Johansen classics—LOVESWEPT hopes to make your holiday very special and very specially romantic.

With every good wish for a holiday filled with the best things in life—the love of family and friends.

Sincerely,

Carolyn Nichols

Carolyn Nichols,
Publisher,
LOVESWEPT
Bantam Books
666 Fifth Avenue
New York, NY 10103

P.S. GIVE YOURSELF A SPECIAL PRESENT: CALL OUR LOVESWEPT LINE 1-900-896-2505 TO HEAR EXCITING NEWS FROM ONE OF YOUR FAVORITE AUTHORS AND TO ENTER OUR SWEEPSTAKES TO WIN A FABULOUS TRIP FOR TWO TO PARIS!

FOREVER LOVESWEPT

SPECIAL KEEPSAKE
EDITION OFFER
12^95^

VALUE

Here's your chance to receive a special hardcover Loveswept "Keepsake Edition" to keep close to your heart forever. Collect hearts (shown on next page) found in the back of Loveswepts #426-#449 (on sale from September 1990 through December 1990). Once you have collected a total of 15 hearts, fill out the coupon and selection form on the next page (no photocopies or hand drawn facsimiles will be accepted) and mail to: Loveswept Keepsake, P.O. Box 9014, Bohemia, NY 11716.

FOREVER LOVESWEPT
SPECIAL KEEPSAKE EDITION OFFER
SELECTION FORM

Choose from these special Loveswepts by your
favorite authors. Please write a 1 next to your first
choice, a 2 next to your second choice. Loveswept
will honor your preference as inventory allows.

_____BAD FOR EACH OTHER   Billie Green

_____NOTORIOUS   Iris Johansen

_____WILD CHILD   Suzanne Forster

_____A WHOLE NEW LIGHT   Sandra Brown

_____HOT TOUCH   Deborah Smith

_____ONCE UPON A TIME...GOLDEN
        THREADS   Kay Hooper

Attached are 15 hearts and the selection form which
indicates my choices for my special hardcover Loveswept
"Keepsake Edition." Please mail my book to:

NAME:_____

ADDRESS:_____

CITY/STATE:_____ ZIP:_____

Offer open only to residents of the United States, Puerto Rico and
Canada. Void where prohibited, taxed, or restricted. Allow 6 - 8
weeks after receipt of coupons for delivery. Offer expires
January 15, 1991. You will receive your first choice as inventory
allows; if that book is no longer available, you'll receive your
second choice, etc.